© Kaito Shibano

"It is I,
Oda
Nobunaga
—your
profession!"

"...Darling, **kill me** for **treason.**"

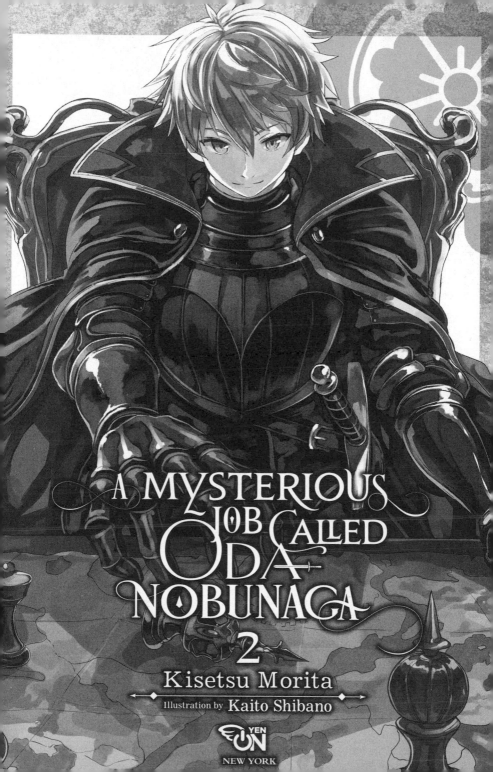

A MYSTERIOUS JOB CALLED ODA NOBUNAGA

2

Kisetsu Morita

Illustration by Kaito Shibano

YEN ON

NEW YORK

A Mysterious Job Called

Oda Nobunaga, Vol. 2

Kisetsu Morita

Translation by Alex Wetnight
Cover art by Kaito Shibano

ODA NOBUNAGA TOIU NAZONO SHOKUGYO GA MAHO KENSHI YORI CHEAT
DATTANODE, OUKOKU WO TSUKURU KOTONI SHIMASHITA volume 2
Copyright © 2017 Kisetsu Morita
Illustrations copyright © 2017 Kaito Shibano
All rights reserved.
Original Japanese edition published in 2017 by SB Creative Corp.

This English edition is published by arrangement with SB Creative Corp., Tokyo in care of
Tuttle-Mori Agency, Inc., Tokyo.

English translation © 2020 by Yen Press, LLC

Yen On
150 West 30th Street, 19th Floor
New York, NY 10001

Visit us at yenpress.com
facebook.com/yenpress
twitter.com/yenpress
yenpress.tumblr.com
instagram.com/yenpress

First Yen On Edition: September 2020

Yen On is an imprint of Yen Press, LLC.
The Yen On name and logo are trademarks of Yen Press, LLC.

The publisher is not responsible for websites (or their content) that are not owned by the
publisher.

Library of Congress Control Number: 2019942581

ISBNs: 978-1-9753-0558-1 (paperback)
       978-1-9753-0559-8 (ebook)

10 9 8 7 6 5 4 3 2 1

LSC-C

Printed in the United States of America

A MYSTERIOUS JOB CALLED ODA NOBUNAGA

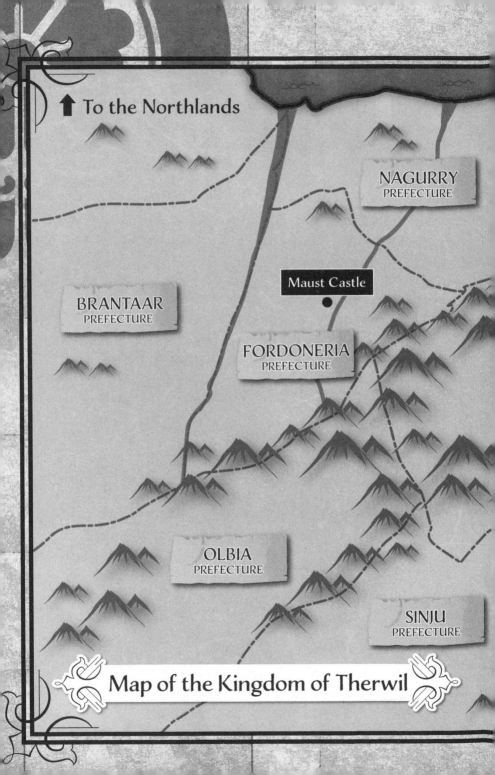

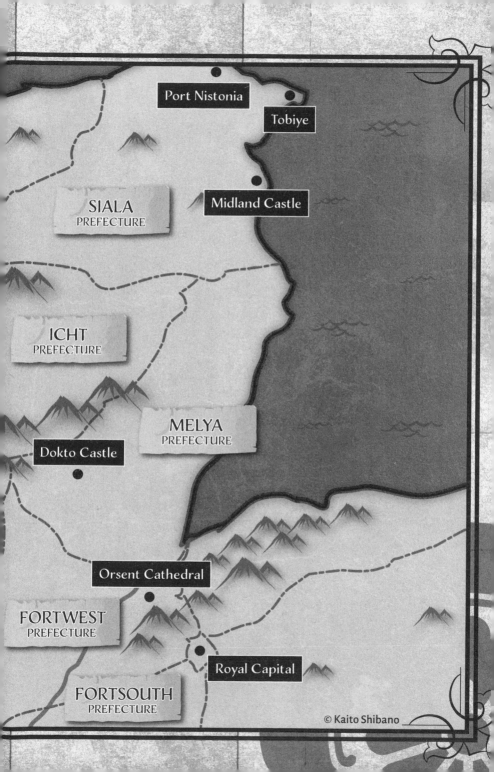

Oda Nobunaga

Mysterious entity and Alsrod's "profession," who often speaks to Alsrod. Is really Oda Nobunaga, a conqueror from another world.

Alsrod Nayvil

Second son of the small Nayvil clan in Fordoneria Prefecture. After succeeding as clan head at the age of eighteen, he quickly expanded his territory and became lord of Fordoneria, Nagurry, and Icht Prefectures.

A MYSTERIOUS JOB CALLED ODA NOBUNAGA

CHARACTER PROFILES

Illustration by Kaito Shibano

Seraphina Caltis

Daughter of Ayles Caltis and Alsrod's official wife. Has the highly rare profession of Saint.

Laviala Aweyu

Alsrod's milk sister and half-elven childhood friend. A well-rounded, good-natured young lady skilled in combat and strategy.

Altia Nayvil

Alsrod's younger sister. Married to Brando Naaham, a minor lord of Olbia Prefecture.

Fleur Wouge

Daughter of a petty lord in northern Fordoneria Prefecture. Became Alsrod's concubine to restore her clan. Talented at her work.

Ayles Caltis

Ruthless leader of Brantaar Prefecture. Allied with Alsrod.

Kelara Hilara

A military officer serving Hasse. Has the profession Akechi Mitsuhide. Now works for Alsrod, who recognized her potential and hired her as one of his vassals.

Lumie

Younger sister of Hasse, who put her into a convent out of fear for her safety during the war.

Hasse

Cousin of the current king and son of the last. Now working to retake the throne with Alsrod's support.

A MYSTERIOUS JOB CALLED ODA NOBUNAGA

CONTENTS

Upon returning to Maust Castle, I paid a visit to Crown Prince Hasse. I'd had a home away from home built in the castle for him, and he and his family were living there now. Incidentally, Hasse had taken the daughter of one of his top vassals as a wife—though not as an official wife. Apparently he wasn't going to take an official wife until he became king. This vassal of his wasn't exactly an influential supporter but rather a member of a clan following Hasse out of necessity.

"Thanks to your guardian knight Kelara, the battle went well for us. You have my gratitude."

"Kelara? Nothing but brains, that woman. I've always heard dwarves were painstaking and diligent, but she's so diligent it's suffocating." Apparently Hasse didn't have a lot of respect for Kelara.

"For me, she is more breathtaking than suffocating. With her knightly physique, she is lovely to watch. I'm jealous that you have someone like her as a vassal."

"You're good at flattery, Count. If you're so enchanted by her, I'll officially hand her over as your vassal."

"With gratitude, sir. I shall grant land to her at once and treat her as a viscount." Personally, I thought Hasse was a man without vision. But thanks to that, I had just gotten my hands on a good general.

As Kelara was a woman, she could enter the consorts' quarters within the castle, so she was able to use her knowledge to help arrange the annual women's functions. Now the castle was just like the royal palace—in presentation at least. The maids also squealed about Kelara's knightly appearance and demeanor—her service to the crown prince did make her seem rather put together.

One day, I called Kelara to my room. I wanted to talk about the next war.

"Next, we'll attack Siala Prefecture. I'm not too worried about the Antoini clan, but there are some powerful lords in that land I want to win over to our side."

"The Nistonia clan, who hold Port Nistonia," Kelara replied immediately. Of course she already knew that much.

"Right. The Nistonias have a powerful navy. From what I hear, with the cooperation of their neighbors, they could bring two hundred ships to bear, which gives them control of the seas. I'm from a landlocked prefecture, so my naval prowess is lacking." I definitely wanted the Nistonias working with me. "I'm confident we could defeat them attacking by land. When the battle is over, though, their navy will be scattered. They can flee by ship, after all. In that case, it's better to bring the Nistonias to our side, here."

The Antoinis had some influence over them, but ultimately the Nistonias were an independent power. I'd been content to ignore them until now, but I might be able to win them over.

Kelara was listening quietly. Her facial expression remained stubbornly neutral; that must've been why Hasse thought she was a bore. Since we each had a unique profession, though, I felt a sort of affinity for her.

"Having a port, the Nistonias must be getting plenty of money from it, too. With the literature they receive from overseas, they have different values from rural nobles—I want you to take advantage of that to convince them with your hospitality."

"My hospitality, sir?"

"That's right. You're the most cultured person in this land. Thanks to your Akechi Mitsuhide profession, you might even be more cultured than anyone in the royal capital. If you show the Nistonias we have the highest cultural standards, I doubt they'll stand a chance."

"Understood. I shall prepare something extraordinary, as if I were entertaining the king himself. If they agree to come, I will make absolutely certain they're satisfied," Kelara replied, nodding.

"Right. I have no doubt you'll succeed. Oh, there was one other thing I wanted from you. Could you come here a second?"

Kelara came over to me quietly, and I gave her a swift kiss on the lips.

"You have peculiar interests, my lord." Kelara's pupils seemed to widen ever so slightly.

"Not at all. I suppose the crown prince wasn't interested in you—what a shame. I've fallen for you."

"I believe the prince was never fond of my race. Elves, dwarves, and beastfolk were never in the royal family's guard in their glory days."

"Were you never mocked for that unusual profession of yours?" I asked.

Kelara had hardly reacted to my kiss, but at that, she grimaced.

"Yes… I was treated quite coldly… The effects of my profession weren't any good for battle, either, so I was told many times I shouldn't be a knight… To be fair, I don't have the skill with a sword or bow to do great deeds, like some hero would."

Kelara's personality didn't make her a bore; she must've been raised in an environment that made her the way she was. No matter how well versed she was in the old ways, somewhere inside she saw herself as a knight, so she'd never been able to feel proud of herself.

"My profession is a bit of an oddity, too, you know. My brother and his lackeys mocked me right after I got it. It was frustrating, but I couldn't talk back to him at the time. Power is the only thing people like that understand." And so I'd shown them. I'd made myself a great lord ruling over three prefectures, including Icht Prefecture. "Serve me; devote yourself to me. I'll ensure your name stays in the history books a thousand years from now."

"Thank you very much." A smile crept its way onto Kelara's face.

And so I made love to her.

"I've studied a bit…about how to please one's partner, too…" Her face red, Kelara toyed with every inch of my body. As inexperienced as she was, she sure did know her stuff.

That night, I was completely enraptured with this brown-skinned dwarf woman.

"I told Laviala there was nothing between us, but I guess that's a lie now..."

"It was true at the time you said it, so I don't think there was any deceit," Kelara said as she lay next to me. Her face already had the look of a knight again. I felt like I had a bodyguard there with me.

◇

Soltis, the head of the Nistonia clan, came with his wife and daughter. He said he'd left his son at home, perhaps fearing an assassination would end his line. Of course, having been asked to come with his family, he couldn't just come by himself. So he brought his women with him. Even in times of war, murdering women is considered uncouth. When a castle fell and its lord was about to die, it was common practice to let the women out alive.

Together with Kelara, I greeted Soltis. Laviala was showing his wife and daughter around.

"Thank you for coming all the way here from so far away. I have been eager to establish friendly relations with your clan. I'd like to introduce you to my vassal Kelara."

Kelara bowed.

"No—thank you. It is an honor to be invited by you and the crown prince..." Soltis was stiff and unsmiling—in fact, he seemed a bit nervous.

"I'm not one to beat around the bush, so I'll be blunt: Did you think you might be assassinated?"

"C-certainly not..."

My asking so directly seemed to have startled him.

"Worry not, for I am a servant of the crown prince. I could never do anything to sully his reputation. If I did, the surrounding lords would all surely leave."

"Right. That is true…"

"First, I would like to present you to the crown prince. Afterward, I shall show you around the castle with Kelara."

Seemingly having settled into his new role, Hasse now acted majestically. The meeting room was filled with expensive furnishings to remind his guests that he was not the crown prince in name only. His seven-year-old daughter was there, too, relieving the tension.

Well, the formalities are over. Now just to follow Kelara's lead.

"My name is Kelara Hilara. First I will now show you to the top floor of the castle, where you will have a good view of the town of Maust."

From the viewing area on the top floor, we indeed had a great view of Maust and all its waterways. Oda Nobunaga had said it looked like a go board, but I didn't know what go was. Maybe it was like chess.

"I've been to the royal capital several times myself, and this place looks like it could be easily mistaken for it…" Soltis seemed astonished, seeing the landscape in a new light.

"Comparing it to the capital would certainly be an exaggeration, but I am honored by your compliment. The population probably exceeds ten thousand."

"Ten thousand… That certainly is a metropolis…"

As my domain had expanded, population growth had accelerated.

"If we were to take in the crown prince, his abode needed to befit him. We're relieved to have our appearances in order. Well, Kelara, show us the next spot."

"Yes, sir, as you wish. Let us proceed to the weapon and armor room."

Where Kelara headed was a collection room of weapons and armor, the room having been established for this day. As my territory had grown, many large temples had become a part of it. Sometimes they'd received offerings of the finest-quality armaments from people praying for victory or whatnot. This was where I displayed them. The floor was covered in a carpet with intricate patterns, too. Together with the arms that adorned it, the room was truly a sight to behold.

"Wow… What a collection…"

"I'm a soldier at the end of the day. Besides, many of my vassals lack any sort of sophistication, so if I collected only paintings and antiques, they would complain that I've gone soft. But for instruments of war, I have an excuse."

"I don't think even the royal palace has this much…"

"Well, I had to collect enough to make this like a palace away from home for the crown prince."

Kelara graciously continued entertaining Soltis—especially at dinner, where all manner of delicacies were brought in and various kinds of alcohol were served.

Kelara poured some liquor for Soltis. "We have an assortment of beverages sourced from many territories. I suspect you'll enjoy comparing the flavors."

"Oh, how very kind of you." He seemed to be gradually starting to relax.

"We will now present you with a performance by several dancers from the royal capital. May I direct your attention forward, please?"

Girls dressed in bright and alluring clothing appeared and began to dance to the sound of a flute. Several layers of thin silk cloth fluttered about, matching with the girls' steps.

"Miss Kelara—and Count Nayvil, too—I've not experienced such luxury in all my life. So this is the authority of someone on par with royalty."

It seemed Soltis had realized our difference in power. There was still something important left, however.

"Come tomorrow, we humbly request that you watch our soldiers as they march. My lord Alsrod is working very hard to give the crown prince a proper escort to the capital," Kelara said in the capital's clear accent.

The next day came.

From high up on the castle, Soltis, seeing the display of my guardsmen as they marched and performed, was literally trembling—or so I heard. Of course, I was watching the performance nearby myself, as my presence helped motivate my men. I heard everything about Soltis from Kelara.

"You can get your troops to move with this much discipline…?" he'd apparently said to her.

And she'd replied, "There is a secret to this."

"And what might that be?"

"My lord has proven himself on many battlefields. He has defeated his enemies with inferior numbers on more than a few occasions. A soldier could not be prouder of fighting for and under the command of such a man. They give their all even during drills."

She said Soltis had gulped at that.

"Also," she'd added, "Siala Prefecture will be on the way as he escorts His Highness to the capital." Right where the Nistonia clan was. "If he had the cooperation of the Nistonias, I think my lord would be most relieved."

Soltis must've understood the threat. However, Kelara was never one to provoke. She'd then respectfully bowed her head.

"As a vassal, it is not my place to say this, but—can I not ask you to lend Alsrod your strength?"

There wasn't a shred of any lie or embellishment to Kelara's story. I knew because right after the dancers' performance the previous day, Soltis had come to me directly and said, "When you come to Siala Prefecture, I shall guide you as head of the Nistonia clan."

"Thank you for choosing to aid the crown prince." I grasped his hand firmly.

Thus, without fighting, the Nistonias and their navy were mine.

Next was a full-on attack on the Antoinis.

Everything was in place. I had Hasse give the order to all lords along the road to Siala Prefecture and the royal capital that they should accompany him. Most of the lords of Siala, including the Antoini clan, refused to comply with what they saw as an invasion. I was fine with that. This war would see all of Siala come under my rule.

My guard troops had grown considerably in number. There were too many for just the Red Bears and the White Eagles, so I established a new unit I named the Black Dogs. As captain of the Black Dogs I appointed Dorbeau, a werewolf from Brantaar Prefecture who'd once run a school for spearmen. He'd later joined the White Eagles and mastered the three-jarg spear before anyone else.

"You are not my soldiers. You are the soldiers of the man who will soon become king. I am but a commander. Keep that in mind as you go to battle."

""Hoorah!!"" Their voices echoed as one. I suppose I do enjoy the battlefield, after all. Of course, I couldn't really be going out on the front line anymore, though.

"Bathe His Highness's enemies in blood! Your heroism will be rewarded!"

""Hoorah!!""

Apparently knowing they were no match, the Sialans decided to abandon their smaller forts and join together with the Antoini clan's main force. Clearly they realized it'd do them no good to be destroyed piecemeal.

Our enemies had reportedly received reinforcements from prefectures besides Siala. Their numbers were too great for a single prefecture otherwise. Our men numbered eight thousand, theirs sixty-five hundred. On the other hand, this meant they were a jumbled assortment of troops. We could win by destroying their coordination.

I didn't act right away. Taking position on a hill, I waited for them. My less numerous opponents set up across from us.

Then, as we stared each other down, I carried on writing letters as if in peacetime. Of course, the subject of those letters was how I'd reward anyone who switched sides. I addressed them to the top vassals of the Antoinis as well as smaller independent lords.

Whether they actually switched sides didn't matter, as my goal was to send them into paranoia. Worrying if their neighbors would betray them would naturally weaken them as they fought.

"Lord Alsrod, you're unusually relaxed," Laviala remarked quizzically.

"What? You think I'm an impatient man?"

"At the very least, you never take your time attacking your enemies, right?"

"It's fine; others are attacking them as we wait. Eventually they won't be able to wait any longer."

"Oh, that's right. The attack from the sea."

Exactly. The eight thousand I mentioned were land troops.

Soltis Nistonia was attacking the Antoinis' coastal stronghold, Tobiye. If they took Tobiye, they could use it as a base to pressure the Antoinis' home castle—popularly known as Midland Castle—farther south. There was no way the Nistonian navy could lose at sea, meaning the fall of Tobiye was virtually certain.

The Antoinis would then have no choice but to return home. However, it'd be impossible for them to withdraw their entire force from my army. They would decide they needed to drive us back with a frontal attack first. That was when I'd crush them.

Five days into the stare down, an envoy came reporting that Tobiye had fallen. I called my generals to a meeting right away.

"The enemy now has no choice but to attack. They will probably charge, so have the archers hit them with concentrated arrows from the forward castles when they do. Then have our crack troops attack with spears. As long as our enemy thinks this is a contest of numbers, we can't lose."

Generally, the side with greater numbers was stronger. But by providing each soldier with the right training and weapons, you could bring out a strength beyond the sum of its parts. And with my numbers being greater than the enemy's, the battle would be decided quickly.

——What an easy fight. Not even a hint of danger.

Oda Nobunaga offered his own opinion of the situation. Honestly, I wasn't going to have any real trouble until I got to the royal capital. The problem would come after I got there—only then would my enemies finally think to work together to attack me. Until I got to the capital, they would all be worried about themselves in the end. Their interests would only coincide when a lord besides themselves had come close to the capital, and they realized they needed to stop it.

There's no one left in my path who can beat me.

——Quite true. Now go and prove to them your soldiers' might.

"When they retreat, ravage them. I'll give three counties to the one who takes their clan leader's head." My generals reacted with great excitement.

◇

And so, just as I'd expected, the enemy attacked head-on. They probably just hoped they could somehow get us to pull back.

——They aren't organized enough. Their leaders command separately, so there's no coordination. What a lost cause.

Oda Nobunaga pointed out their faults. He was exactly right; the enemy was old-fashioned. They couldn't contend with modern military tactics.

From a forward castle on high ground, Laviala shouted, "Everyone fire!" She simultaneously lowered a big red flag. A volley of arrows went flying, reducing the attacking enemy numbers from far away.

After three or so more such volleys, our spearmen plunged in from the front. Their long three-jarg spears shattered enemy skulls, whether they were protected by heavy iron helmets or not, and the dead soldiers collapsed straight to the ground.

If the enemy's momentum stopped, we were at a total advantage simply from having greater numbers. The tide of battle had quickly become one-sided.

"Kelara's deliberately targeting the weaker lords," I noted. Once those fell back, the other soldiers would likewise try to fall back before anyone else. They'd be impossible to control. Noen Rowd and Meissel Wouge's troops were doing well driving them back, too. "All right, let's see if they can take the enemy general's head."

——The odds of the commanding general dying on the battlefield are extremely low. I wouldn't get your hopes up.

Thanks.

In the end, the Antoini army was completely routed, and it returned to their home castle. However, given their utter inability to defend it, this too they abandoned, fleeing into the arms of Melya, the neighboring prefecture to the south.

Driving out the remaining resistance in Siala, I had now unified this prefecture as well.

◇

The real hero of this war was Soltis Nistonia. I granted him as territory two neighboring counties and a few outlying areas.

Returning to Maust, I reported my subjugation of Siala to Hasse.

"The terrain makes it difficult to march on the royal capital from the north, so let us use the traditional entrance from Fortsouth Prefecture. All that stands in our way to the capital now are Melya and Fortsouth Prefectures. The most capable lords of the Melya clan and Fortsouth's Santira clan are gathering. Still, as for whether they can stand against us, I do not think they will be a problem."

In the cardinal directions around the capital were four prefectures, and although they were among the few highly populated regions of the kingdom, as was the capital itself, the south side was more developed than the north. So entering from the south was the precedent, aside from some surprise attacks.

Rather than there being a single owner of the prefecture, though, it was held in separate parts, mostly by top vassals who'd been given land one by one because of their close relations with the royal family.

In the past, no one had supposed a powerful lord would cause a big rebellion, so the top vassals hadn't been given that much land. The rebellions of powerful lords could be defeated by other powerful lords along with the king's personal troops. However, once the realm's lords stopped obeying the king, and the commanders of his personal troops started acting according to their own will, the military power of the royal family had come close to zero. They had kept up appearances by depending on lords who did have power.

"Well done! Getting to the capital is just a matter of time now!" Hasse said. Unifying Siala had brought us much closer to getting to the capital.

"I am currently trying to convince the lords of Fortsouth to join our side. If they do, you will instantly be able to enter the capital like a king, with your head held high."

The capital was militarily difficult to defend. It was originally a walled city, but with the rising population, people had begun living on the outside, and parts of the wall had been destroyed. Trying to defend outside the city, and fleeing to the countryside if unsuccessful, had been the way of things for the past several generations of kings. Even if they had tried to fight to the end inside the castle, the capital would have been destroyed. None of the capital residents would have recognized a king who'd made such a decision, and without the support of their subjects, they wouldn't have been able to rule their land any longer.

"We've practically already won. It'd be nice if my cousin Paffus just handed over the throne. He shouldn't make my subjects throw away their lives needlessly." Hasse was clearly already king in his own mind. Of course, if we didn't make that a reality, there would be problems.

"At present, it seems the king intends to fend off our forces with all his might," I informed Hasse.

"Hmph. He doesn't know when to give up…"

"Of course, that is his intention—nothing more." I brought Hasse a few letters. "Gradually, more and more people are trying to join our side. As they do, eventually the king must give up and flee to some lord far away."

"Ah! Quite good, quite good."

"To accelerate this process, let us hold out rewards and promises of land to entice more to our side. Likewise, I shall encourage the king to abdicate."

"I see, I see!" Hasse's voice was getting louder and louder; apparently, he was in a very good mood. "But speaking of rewards, I must give you one first."

"That is most generous of you."

"You already have more land than anyone except those on the frontier. It's time you carried the title of marquess, not count."

Indeed, being a marquess might be an effective way to help suppress my enemies. Marquess could for all intents and purposes be called the highest rank attainable for a vassal, given only to the king's advisers.

"Yes, my liege. I humbly accept."

"And there's been another happy event in your life, I hear. It seems your concubine is with child, yes? How wonderful." Fleur, the sister of my general Meissel Wouge and my concubine, had sent word of her pregnancy the other day. Hopefully her child would be just as healthy as Seraphina's and Laviala's children. "Here, I want you to have this cooking playset that was passed down in the royal family. It's intricately made from wood; the food looks like smaller versions of the real thing."

"I will gratefully accept that as well."

My title therein changed from Count of Fordoneria to Marquess of Fordoneria. In the castle town, since I lived in a castle surrounded by water, apparently people called me the water fortress marquess.

Now there was still a bit more I needed to do.

I went out to the rear courtyard at night, where I was greeted by fourteen or so wolves. They weren't exactly my pets—although you could say I'd practically hand-raised them.

They were the *rappas*. I'd been putting them to work frequently, and gradually their number had grown. No longer with their original master—my financial officer Fanneria—they were now officers under my personal command.

"Find out if the lesser lords of Siala intend to obey my orders and report back to me," I instructed.

One wolf with especially nice fur stepped forward. "Go ahead," I told them. "You may speak."

At that, the wolf changed into humanoid form. It was a young female werewolf. Her hair was trimmed to an even length just so it touched her shoulders, maybe to keep it out of her face.

"What is it, Yadoriggy?" Even I didn't know her real name.

"Is it all right to dispose of anyone who's clearly useless?"

"Yes, but no more than two. No, actually, maybe it's safer to take out the trash first...? Do as you please."

"As you wish," Yadoriggy replied succinctly. "I suspect the people of Siala don't understand the position they're in. They would probably side with the Melyans if their forces came."

"Probably. I'd like to pacify them before getting to the royal capital. Is there anyone who'd be fit to govern them?"

"If that prefecture is the front line, perhaps Sir Kivik?"

"Very well. I'll think about it."

An elder even among my commanders, Kivik had also been the first person to recognize my talents and serve me. We had put our lives on the line fighting together at Fort Nagraad as well. Maybe being in a place where war could break out anytime better suited his personality. Yadoriggy certainly wasn't wrong there, and I doubted anyone would be envious of Kivik, either.

Yadoriggy returned to her wolf form, and the wolves dispersed to their respective destinations.

The crown prince might have wanted to go to the capital right away, but a rebellion on the way back to Maust would only dampen our spirits.

Later, per Yadoriggy's suggestion, I made Kivik a viscount of five counties in Siala.

"I thought this might be better for you than somewhere too peaceful, so I've entrusted it to you. Make it just as peaceful as Nayvil."

"Oh, I wasn't aware there were five extra counties in Siala." Stroking his white beard, Kivik wore a blank expression on his face. To be sure, there wasn't much left after summing those five counties and Soltis Nistonia's domain.

"I'm transferring land from some other lords. They aren't terribly powerful, after all. It's not a problem. In fact, it'd be simpler if they did rebel."

"I see. In that case, I must agree that I should go."

"Leave your home base to Little Kivik. I bet he'd like to finally be away from his father, too, and finally have some peace and quiet." Little Kivik was a good age himself, but with his spry father still active and never retiring, he didn't seem like the head of his clan.

"Perhaps. I'll be wary of the Antoini remnants that fled to Melya, too."

Of course, I had put thought into whom I'd chosen. "Let's take some time for things to quiet down. I'm concerned about going to the capital too quickly. I'm sure the people there would see me as just some bizarre young upstart anyway."

I'm still just a bit over twenty years old. The public would only find the mysteries around me unsettling. Not that I particularly care what they think of me, but a rebellion would not be productive.

——Good decision. Kiso Yoshinaka was also surprisingly unpopular in the capital, leading to his demise. You ought to carefully consider when you go.

He mentioned yet another name I'd never heard of, but even in my world, there had been a warlord who'd captured the capital with a large army only to lose it, and his life, two months later.

Without enough food, taking the capital with a large force means your men have to loot. It's impossible to rule when you've made all the residents your enemies.

——Precisely. You've still only lived half as long as I did. You have time. The hastier you are the sooner your end will come.

It was a bit odd to hear a conqueror advise caution, but any king, even a demon king, would want to hold on to his power as long as possible.

◇

Before Kivik arrived in Siala, two petty lords who'd been offering their allegiance died mysteriously. I could only think the rappas had killed them. Apparently their families believed it was murder as well. The dead lords' clans holed up in castles and rebelled, so I sent Kivik and put them down. Other than holding their land for generations, they were an entirely uninteresting lot. Melyan troops attacked Kivik a few times, but they were all just skirmishes.

Yadoriggy advised me on where I should attack next. At the time, she was dressed as a werewolf dancer—such a sight wasn't uncommon in a castle. Besides, by looking like a dancer, she could travel the land with a troupe of performers, and nobody would raise an eyebrow.

"I'm sure you know the Melya clan's vassals hold a substantial share of the power," she said.

"I do. They always decide things by council. It's even written into their laws."

——Hmm, just like the Rokkaku.

Apparently, Oda Nobunaga was familiar with the arrangement, too. Lords who were controlled by their vassals probably existed everywhere.

"Word is the clan head, Xylan Melya, is trying to rein them in, causing them to butt heads. It seems Xylan believes the only option is to submit to you."

Well, with only one prefecture under his thumb, he probably knew he couldn't beat me.

"Tell them this: For my part, I won't bring them to harm if they hand over the Antoinis."

"As you wish."

"Oh, and tell them to ensure Xylan's vassals find out. This should not be a secret."

"As you wish."

That way, baseless though it was, they'd quarrel among themselves. And that would work in my favor. There were other ways to suppress your enemies besides war.

"Additionally," she said, "one of us managed to sneak into Orsent Cathedral in Fortwest Prefecture, and they say the archbishop there wouldn't mind siding with you."

Fortwest Prefecture was essentially controlled by Orsent Cathedral. There were individual lords in place, but they held almost no power.

"I see. I need to think of how to prepare for my capital entrance soon. I don't want to bring shame on myself." Governance would be impossible if I didn't know anything about the capital. I needed time to study.

"I'm afraid I don't know anything about that," Yadoriggy said, bowing her head.

"That's fine. Everyone has their role. I'll ask Kelara."

For about a half year afterward, I settled down, from other people's point of view. I celebrated my twenty-third birthday in a time of peace and quiet. I didn't look much different, but my son and daughter certainly did. They would both run about the castle corridors, driving their wet nurse Laviala crazy.

I wasn't exactly slacking, though. With Kelara's help, I meticulously researched the rituals and political affairs of the capital as well as the values of its people. The crown prince Hasse would be king, but I would be the one running the government.

"I'm impressed by how devoted you are to your studies." Even Kelara was shocked that I went so far as to take notes—not that her face showed much shock.

"I don't want anyone to think I'm just some country boy. For one thing, there's nothing more aggravating than being mocked by incompetent fools, and if my reputation suffered, some people might try to bring back Paffus VI after he's gone."

Quite a few people had taken control of the capital in the past, but very few had managed to keep it under their rule with any stability. It was all due to their ignorance about the capital. There existed no precedent for a city that purportedly had thirty or forty thousand inhabitants. As a result, concentrated into this one place was a tangled web of special interests.

"I see. I shall do everything in my power to impart my knowledge to you." Kelara never batted an eye. I could see why the crown prince said she was unwavering and stiff, but that was precisely what was so reassuring about her. Part of what showed a ruler's skills was how they made use of their vassals. "Well then, today let's talk about commerce in the capital," she continued.

"Oh, no, that's enough studies for tonight." I went up to Kelara and wrapped my arms around her. "Making love to a woman like a country boy won't do. Teach me what you know."

"As you wish."

With a straight face, she took off her clothes, exposing her brown skin to me. Her silver hair seemed more radiant than ever.

◇

The day after bedding Kelara, I became father to a third child. Fleur had given birth to a girl.

Fleur was a brave woman, and apparently that hadn't changed even in childbirth; according to those present, she hardly looked in pain at all. They said they'd never seen such a quiet birth.

"You must be exhausted, Fleur." When I went to see Fleur where she still lay in bed, she seemed unconcerned, as if she'd just had a bit of a cold.

"After everything I've heard about the pain of childbirth, I was expecting it to be far more difficult than it was."

"I almost feel like I'm hearing a warrior bragging."

"Thinking about the survival of my clan was much harder." She wasn't smiling, which told me she was completely sincere.

"The Wouge clan isn't going anywhere now, so just worry about whether our daughter grows up healthy. Let's get someone trustworthy to be her nurse, too."

"Yes, my lord. I will make certain your daughter is raised well."

After stroking Fleur's pink hair, I left the room.

And then, as we were holding private celebrations, there was a stir. Our neighbor Melya was reportedly engaged in a civil war. Now there was an opportunity knocking. Sometimes all it took was a little waiting for opportunities to crop up.

◇

A wolf instantly appeared before me when I went to the courtyard that night, and she quickly changed form to the rappa Yadoriggy. The shorter an exchange with a rappa was the better.

"The count who controlled Melya Prefecture, Xylan Melya, purged one of his top vassals for insolence; some of the others retaliated, so he fled his castle, and they are now locked in battle. Xylan has his supporters, too, so the prefecture is broken into two camps."

"Let Kivik know right away. And go tell Xylan that Alsrod is ready to give him protection."

"With Xylan himself already sheltering the Antoinis, I doubt he can officially come to our side."

Indecisive bastard. He'd decided he was no match for me, and yet he still harbored the Antoinis, who had defied and fled from me. It was little surprise his vassals had disobeyed such a fickle count.

"Tell Xylan any friend of the Antoinis is my enemy." I'd make him see he had no options. I gave instructions to my troops to be ready to move out at a moment's notice.

And finally, Xylan sent an envoy requesting troops to retake Melya. With the attacks against Xylan gradually getting more intense, he seemed to be in dire straits.

Xylan's vassals had set up his younger brother Salhorn as a puppet ruler. Melya Prefecture was completely rent in two. Family squabbles weren't too uncommon, but now there was a lord waiting to take advantage of all of this, right here. If he had a problem, that was it.

The time had come. I headed straight to Hasse.

"Now more than ever, please lend me your strength. The time for you to be king has drawn near."

Hasse agreed to my plan right away.

And so an army ten thousand strong marched from Maust. I, however, was not the commanding general.

It was the crown prince, Hasse.

I was right next to him, but he was the one in charge.

"Listen up!" he said. "I want you all to eliminate the treacherous vassals attacking Count Xylan Melya! Melya Prefecture is close to the royal capital. We cannot sit by and watch such chaos go on so close to our borders! Anyone who defies me is a traitor against the royal family!"

Since he hadn't been to battle for a long time, Hasse's voice was shrill, but with his goal so close, he looked excited.

If Crown Prince Hasse made an appearance here, the king in control of the capital would have no choice but to side with the Melya clan's vassals. Surely he couldn't side with his cousin who claimed to be the crown prince. This situation would escalate beyond Melya's problem.

I trusted the werewolf captain of the Black Dogs, Dorbeau, to be the vanguard this time. I told him to crush our enemies without mercy.

Even with reinforcements from the Santira clan in Fortsouth Prefecture, our enemy numbered five thousand at most. On the other hand, we had ten thousand, and if you added Xylan's troops, we had an even greater number advantage.

Opting not to be sieged, our enemy struck out onto the plains. Since holing up in a castle with five thousand men would be next to impossible, they must've had no choice. Besides, while they were slowly besieged in their base, Xylan would be rallying his men.

After clashing once with the enemy, Captain Dorbeau of the Black Dogs deliberately pulled back, causing the enemy line to stretch. His strategy was to then make another attack on their flank and destroy them. It was a swift attack befitting a werewolf. The plan worked—the enemy routed and withdrew.

You could say the first round, at least, had gone to us. The enemy ultimately changed their plan to splitting up and defending multiple castles. Their morale had been damaged somewhat.

"At this rate, do you think the battle will drag on?" Laviala asked me that night. We were in a room of the mansion I was using as my quarters. A strategic map was on the table.

"Not at all. Right about now there's another task force heading to attack their main castle."

"Another task force? That's the first I've heard…"

"Because I made sure not to tell you. If all our troops know, the enemy will find out, too."

"Still, at least tell *me* about it…"

"I have a few reasons. The men will be more enthusiastic if they think they're in the main attack. Right about now, Kivik is ravaging Melya Prefecture with two thousand men, behind their lines. Most of our enemies here won't have anywhere to return to."

Laviala let out an "Ahh!" at that. "Speaking of which, you didn't move your troops through Kivik's territory on the way… I thought maybe you wanted him to focus on managing his land…"

"Right now, a lot of the soldiers in the enemy's main stronghold, Dokto Castle, are gone, so it isn't at full strength. We'll take advantage and capture it with a surprise attack by Kivik."

I took game pieces from both sides of the map and moved them closer to the enemy pieces. "Then, together with Kivik, we'll pulverize the enemy troops out confronting us. With that, the Melya clan will effectively be obliterated. We can't kill Xylan Melya since he came to us for help—but at best he'll be living as our puppet."

I moved the piece representing my troops farther in. "This isn't a war about what to do with Melya Prefecture— We'll be taking the royal capital soon. More people are joining our side. The opportunity is ripe."

During the past half year, I'd been scheming to bring more people to my side. It would all now come to fruition.

◇

The next day, my troops began taking the enemy's castles one by one. As usual, I had everyone in the first castle killed as proof of my lack of mercy for those who didn't surrender beforehand. By planting a seed of fear, I robbed them of motivation. At the same time, by having Hasse repeatedly say they were rebelling against the crown prince, I made their position even more precarious. They'd soon realize, the way things were going, Hasse was to become the new king. Opposing him would make things worse and worse for them.

In the midst of all this, a messenger on horseback came to my encampment. They said the Melya clan's stronghold, Dokto Castle, had fallen to Kivik's attack, and Salhorn Melya, who called himself the clan head, had escaped to the royal capital.

"Fool. He should've at least escaped to his own troops. He doesn't even have the courage for that?"

That same day, I announced that Kivik had taken down the enemy's main castle.

"I neglected to mention this before, but that old soldier is my comrade from when I was at Fort Nagraad," I told my men. "I wanted to give him the honor of leading the way to the capital." My generals lit up at the mention of the capital. "This prefecture is just the beginning. Now we head to the capital to make the crown prince king!"

""Whooooo!"" A loud cry went out from among my generals. I'd been making them wait so long for this.

"I'm sure many of you wondered when we were ever going to set our sights on it. I was gathering our strength bit by bit. Under his watch, Kivik did a splendid job stabilizing Siala in almost no time. There's nothing to be afraid of now! Today and tomorrow, we shall obliterate what's left of the enemy!"

Of course, there was no one left following the Melya clan's vassals, so people kept coming to surrender. On the other hand, I let all the ones still resisting have their warriors' deaths. If they meant to die, nothing would convince them otherwise.

Apparently the remnants fled to the royal capital together with an Antoini who used to be a lord in Siala. I don't envy his life as a fugitive.

Two days later, I went into the castle town of the Melya clan's burned-down home, Dokto Castle. Building a temporary shack at the castle ruins, I decided to appoint a castle commander. They'd have the important role of guarding our rear as we invaded farther.

I called Laviala to my quarters.

"I'd like for you to guard this place."

"Lord Alsrod, allow me to set a condition, if I may."

Looking at her face, I could tell right away this was something she absolutely wouldn't compromise on. I'd been with her all my life—ever since the day I was born. We could hide almost nothing from each other.

"I can hazard a guess what you want to say, but tell me anyway."

"I want to be with you as you occupy the royal palace! When will such a momentous day ever come again?"

I knew it. That was exactly what I expected.

"Occupying the palace isn't my goal here. I'm sure you know that."

Becoming king—that was what I desired. I didn't need to put it all into words.

"Still, I want to share the joy of this milestone by your side. I know how important defending Dokto Castle is, but…"

I sighed. To be honest, I'd wanted to share that joy with Laviala, too.

"I want to reward my guardsmen by taking them all with me, too. Maybe I'll let Noen Rowd handle this. He's better at defending than attacking anyway."

Next I summoned Kelara to my quarters.

"Help me make sure I don't do anything embarrassing when we occupy the capital. I can't be bringing shame on His Royal Highness."

"Very well. First, it's crucial you make sure everyone knows it's strictly forbidden to loot."

I was a bit disappointed. "That's the same no matter whose land you're taking. I'm asking more about etiquette."

"May I speak freely, sir?"

I was almost a bit frightened by that, but I told her to hold nothing back. If I got a scathing criticism now, it would sting no matter who I was.

"You were already conscious of etiquette while in Maust. If you continue as you have been, there shouldn't be any problem. You would already make a fine regent for this country, one that nobody could speak ill of."

I was stunned. "Kelara, I never meant you to be a sly little sycophant."

"I have never studied sycophancy, so that's beyond my depth," Kelara responded dryly.

"No matter what you say, my affection for you will never fade."

"I don't mean to belabor this point, but I speak as a vassal—not as your wife."

I couldn't believe she could say such things with such a neutral expression.

"Fine. I trust you. I'll take your word for it."

"Thank you very much. I promise you my undying loyalty, as well, my lord."

Kelara nodded, still not smiling. *Hasse really was a fool to let this one go*, I thought. A person who couldn't tell who was useful couldn't be a good king.

Well, for now I'd just send orders to the surrounding lords to accompany the crown prince. That way it would be crystal clear who was friend and who was foe.

I marched my troops through Fortwest Prefecture and on to Fortsouth Prefecture. I'd received permission of passage from Orsent Cathedral in Fortwest, so although this was a detour, it was at least reliable. Entering the royal capital from Fortsouth was the proper route according to old custom as well.

The surrounding lords rushed to join me.

"Thank you for coming. However, it's pointless to bow your heads to me. I ask that you bow before His Royal Highness, the crown prince. He is the one you will serve, after all."

The greatest power in Fortsouth—our capital entrance—had been the Santira clan, but apparently they'd already lost their will to fight, and their vassals and clan members came to surrender one after another. There was no way they could wage a proper war now. The clan head, Leggus Santira, had fled.

Even the people of the royal capital seemed to realize defense was impossible now; King Paffus VI was said to have fled westward with his clan. He'd probably continue calling himself king, but abandoning the capital would leave a terrible impression.

Hasse would have no trouble going from crown prince to sovereign.

Shattering what pitiful resistance remained, I easily liberated Fortsouth Prefecture. All obstacles to the capital were now gone. It didn't seem there would be any more real battles, so I had my formal attire sent from Maust. Might as well look the part when I took the castle.

I was pretty happy myself, but someone else was even happier.

That person was Crown Prince Hasse.

"This is all because of you, Marquess. I don't know how to express my gratitude... Thank you, thank you..."

As he broke into tears, I wasn't sure how to react.

"Your Royal Highness, could emotions perhaps wait until after we have taken the capital?"

"Oh, I just wanted to let you know how thankful I was. Naturally, I'll thank you after we take it, too. I promise you the position of regent as well."

I couldn't ignore those words.

Regent—arguably the highest position in the kingdom after the king's, it was the highest vassal rank; historically, too, it was the rank that had been attained by various de facto supreme rulers of their times.

"I would be most honored to be your regent. I shall strive to be worthy of the role to do my utmost to ensure peace in the kingdom."

"Yes—and I shall not go back on my promise."

It had taken time, but I was finally here. I was another step closer to my dream of being king.

Well, perhaps it hadn't taken so much time. The position of regent had been handed to me on a silver platter.

I entered the undefended royal capital with thirteen thousand troops.

In front were Kivik's men. As I wasn't a lord or much of anything by birth, my milk sister Laviala was the only vassal who had always been with me. Kivik was therefore my second-longest-serving vassal. He'd had faith in me before I was anyone important; his service was sincere. I'd reasoned that if I was going to reward that loyalty, this was the time to do it.

My guardsmen followed after Kivik, and I followed on my horse.

Special ability Conqueror's Presence acquired.
Takes effect when recognized as a conqueror by many at once. All abilities are tripled from the usual.
Additionally, all who lay eyes on you experience either awe or fear.

Abilities tripled?! What an incredible power. No country has a commander like that.

Of course, since I was going to be regent, I might need that much power.

The Kingdom of Therwil would be mine to rule.

Onlookers—tons of them, since this was the capital—were gathered on both sides of the road. I could hear their hushed voices.

"So that's Marquess Alsrod Nayvil."

"What a bold young man."

"Word is he's only twenty-three."

"They say he's a genius of war."

"Even better, I heard he made his land very rich."

My reputation was outstanding. I had been rather careful about the occupation, after all.

A resplendent and ostentatious carriage came up from behind me. Crown Prince Hasse and his family were riding inside. It wasn't ideal to show the royal family to the masses, and besides, even if I could defend myself against an assassin's arrow, it'd be impossible for Hasse to do the same. Thus, I'd put them in a carriage.

The vassals still in the royal palace prostrated themselves and welcomed us in. They were the officials, bureaucrats, and nobles who weren't strongly tied to either royal line. Rather than fleeing the capital with Paffus VI, they'd stayed to recognize Hasse as the new king. Also included were those who'd been hiding out after getting on Paffus VI's bad side. People who'd been instrumental during the time of Hasse's father, Grandora III, were back, thinking they could return to power.

That day, Hasse entered the castle with a certain level of ceremony, and perhaps unsurprisingly, he wept with emotion. For Hasse, this was a long-awaited return home.

Even though I was using him, I felt like I had done a good deed as I watched.

The next morning, Hasse's coronation ceremony was held in the capital's Therwil Cathedral, which had the most authority in all the kingdom. Our story was that Paffus VI had merely been calling himself king, so by excluding him from the number of kings, Hasse was succeeding his father, Grandora III. These facades were so much extra work, but future historians would decide for us the real order of succession.

Thus, the new king, Hasse I, was born.

——Ah, the conquest of a capital is a sweet victory indeed. I was just as thrilled when I took Kyoto myself.

Oda Nobunaga seemed to be enjoying himself even more than usual. *But your conquest wasn't always smooth sailing, was it? I don't want to find myself in trouble one of these days.*

——If nothing else, you'll be butting heads with Hasse before long. He's the king; he will want all the power for himself. When that happens, your fate will depend on how you handle it.

I guess a honeymoon can't go on forever, huh?

——There's something a bit different about this from my time, though. The former king, that Paffus fellow, is still alive. In that case, this Hasse will have to depend on you. For me, the former shogun, Yoshihide, simply died.

Interesting. So if I side with Paffus, that alone would put Hasse in a crisis. I'd have to keep that in mind. It could be key.

The day after the coronation celebrations were over, I was formally appointed as regent. Naturally, I was the first in the Nayvil clan to reach such a rank. No one else had even advanced past viscount.

"I shall do everything in my power for the glory of Therwil."

That was no lie—but that glorious kingdom was going to be mine someday.

"Sir Regent, if you have any desire at all, name it. As king, I would like to grant your wishes as soon as possible," the new king said generously.

"Well, I would like to have a few cities as my personal territory."

I would gather wealth for myself. Everything that followed would go more smoothly.

"Very well. Would you also take a look at my ideas for which new lords to appoint?"

"Certainly. That would be my duty as regent."

There were more people from the old nobility—the ones who hadn't even supported Hasse—than I'd expected. This man really didn't understand his position.

"Your Majesty, it would be better to reward those who long served you in war and politics. Would the people who only finally returned come with you if you were ever forced out of the capital?"

"I see... You're right, Sir Regent... However, I can't quite give all the land to just your vassals, either..."

Apparently Hasse had expected I might complain.

"Yes, but if you do not place trustworthy people in the capital's vicinity, you will be in danger should Lord Paffus attack. This is not a time of peace. Please understand we are at war. I am not asking you to show favor to my vassals. I am saying that you must be prepared for the enemy and his plans."

"R-right... When you put it that way... People who don't know war would hardly serve as a wall if I put them nearby..."

It looked like I could get him to distribute the new lords in a way that was quite convenient for me. The right words for convincing Hasse naturally came to mind. Maybe this was the work of that Conqueror's Presence ability. Right now, most of the capital's inhabitants saw me—and definitely not Hasse—as a conqueror.

He questioned me about several other important problems. I answered them all very carefully. Because of my position, I couldn't ignore state politics, so it was what I had to do. I needed to balance that well with furthering my own interests.

However, one of those questions was a bit unexpected.

"Sir Alsrod, because of you, I was able to become king and then make you regent. Once again, I thank you," Hasse said, although it seemed the time for such thanks had passed.

"Not at all. That was the plan from the beginning."

Just what was he getting ready to say?

"And so I can finally speak freely with you about my marriage proposal."

"Marriage proposal?"

"My sister, who can only remember life as a wanderer. She'll be thirteen. Will you not take my sister as your official wife?"

Even I hadn't expected that...

To be honest, I was at a total loss. If he'd been asking me to take his vassal's daughter or sister as concubine, I wouldn't have even been surprised. This, however, was a different story altogether.

"Your Majesty, I already have Marquess Ayles Caltis's daughter Seraphina as my official wife... Therefore, I am afraid this proposal to take your sister as my wife would be impossible..."

"She's the daughter of a marquess. This is the king's sister. Her rank alone is obviously higher than your wife's now. In my days as a wanderer, it always saddened me to think I'd have to give her away to some nobody, but now I can give her to you with no regrets. It would make my late father very happy."

The new king Hasse would not give up on this idea so easily. What a mess...

"If you marry my sister, you'll be my brother-in-law, and I would very much like you to become a relative of the royal family."

That certainly was a good offer.

Hasse himself must have realized that I, the manager of all his affairs, would come to have tremendous power, so he probably wanted to keep me in check by making me like a brother.

I wouldn't say it to his face, but there was something in it for me, too. If she and I had a baby, that child would have royal blood. That'd be powerful justification when I founded a new dynasty.

But how would Seraphina feel about all this...? Not happy, certainly. I couldn't bear to break my wife's heart with a political move. Normally when one married a woman of such obviously high stature, the original wife was subsequently treated as a concubine. How humiliating for Seraphina.

"Your Majesty, if you say your sister is still thirteen years old, then surely there is no need to rush. She would not have even had her profession-bestowal ceremony yet. Waiting for that would still leave plenty of time..."

"If I were not king and still living in obscurity, I would have done so, but now you are regent. It seems natural to me that we bind ourselves together with marriage ties."

What was I to do? He had the better argument. Besides, depending on the situation, I might be able to usurp without inviting hatred for overthrowing the royal family by force. This could be a shortcut to my goal.

Still, how should I explain this to Seraphina? Surely she wanted her own child to be king, too. What woman wouldn't want that?

"A-anyway...Your Majesty has only just become king, and I have only just become regent... We need not rush... Besides, there are still many around the capital who don't think too kindly of us—we will still have plenty of time after we've finished subjugating them."

That was a fact. Even supposing no one came to make a surprise attack, there were people keeping a watchful eye on us, including the supporters of the former king, Paffus VI.

"Very well. We'll set this discussion aside for now. But do give it some thought, Sir Regent."

"Actually, Your Majesty, you should think about getting married yourself."

Hasse had both wives and children, but they were the sisters of vassals or the daughters of lords he had stayed with during his travels, so they were too low socially for any to be his official wife.

"True... But your daughter is too young still, and your sister is married. Let's see, who would be suitable...?"

Good, I got him to change the subject.

Seraphina was actually supposed to be coming to the capital from Maust soon. Maybe I'd casually bring it up then to see her reaction...

◇

As I couldn't leave the capital for some time, my wife Seraphina came with a lady-in-waiting. Fleur had only just given birth, so she was still recuperating at Maust.

As the regent's wife, Seraphina adorned herself in the fanciest dress she'd ever worn. There was currently no woman more powerful than her in all the kingdom.

"You look even more handsome as a regent, darling," Seraphina complimented me teasingly when I saw her.

"That might be my profession's fault. It seems to enhance my charisma the higher my position gets."

"How's this, darling? You don't think anyone in the capital will laugh at me with this on, do you?" She spun around once in front of me, her dress fluttering slightly. It was like a great flower had burst into bloom.

"Nobody would be brave enough to laugh at you now, Seraphina."

"Also true. You know, coming to the capital was my dream, since my home was so far away. I studied the monarchy, but putting that knowledge to use in the countryside means something different from in the capital."

Instead of being intimidated by this unfamiliar capital, Seraphina appeared entirely unbothered. *Valiant* was a word most often used to describe warriors, but Seraphina had it in her, too.

"Seraphina, I know this is rather sudden, but there's something I want to tell you. It's about politics. A new problem has arisen since I've arrived here."

"Of course; I'm your wife. I'm glad to hear my husband's troubles."

That night, I visited Seraphina's quarters. First I discussed plans to exterminate the lords rebelling against the new king as well as whom to send as overseer for the cities now under my personal control and so forth.

Even with things I more or less knew the answer to, Seraphina sometimes gave suggestions from a different perspective, so it was actually quite helpful. Hearing about people's reputations among the court ladies was particularly useful. That was basically an indicator of whether the people I mentioned were refined and sophisticated. Locally powerful merchants and creative eccentrics abounded in the cities around the capital. Appointing someone uncivilized as overseer would risk mockery from the merchants and a loss of respect.

"That Kelara girl is head and shoulders above the rest when it comes to old customs. And her table manners are just perfect," said Seraphina. "Still, it'd be a waste of talent to make her overseer of just one city."

"Good point. Maybe I'll ask Fanneria; he used to be a merchant."

"But he was a *rural* merchant. I don't think he could contend with the real merchants in the capital."

"A harsh assessment. But I guess someone who's lived in the capital would be better in a ruthless competition."

We had a lively conversation, as always. As it went on, I kept looking for a chance to bring up what I really wanted to talk about.

"Also, His Majesty said something to me...which I genuinely want your opinion on."

"So now comes the real topic of the day, huh? Go on, tell me."

Realizing this was an important conversation, Seraphina actually leaned in excitedly. Wishing I didn't have to disappoint her, I gazed intently into her eyes as I explained the situation. Without any change of expression, Seraphina stared back into my eyes as she listened.

"...And that's everything. Honestly, I'd really like him to drop it myself. I already have a wife."

"Why does that bother you so much, darling?" Seraphina asked, undaunted.

Of course. I should've just turned him down.

"You should absolutely accept his proposal! Power will just fall into your lap!" Seraphina exclaimed, grasping my hand tightly.

"Huh?! You don't mind...?"

"I told you I want to be a hero's wife. That won't change as a concubine, and I won't be any less powerful. In fact, I can't wait to guide someone so young."

That convinced me—Seraphina really was valiant. Her father, Ayles Caltis, had called her wild. She might've been even more ambitious than I was.

Next, I discussed my concerns about this marriage with the king's sister. I could now focus more on the political side of it than on Seraphina's feelings, so that was a relief.

"But if I have a child with her, yours might never be king. Any child with royal blood comes first in the line of succession."

"I told you before. If my child isn't meant to be king, then he doesn't need to be," Seraphina said without hesitating. "I'll support you on your way to becoming a hero; that's why I married you. So it should be obvious what you need to do."

When she put it that way, the answer was pretty clear.

"You're right. Paffus's cronies are still everywhere. Until we quash them all, it'd be better to have close ties with the king."

Lots of people had held power as regent. But pretty much none of them had managed to hold on to it, because the people who wanted them gone always conspired against them. The previous regents had had especially little in terms of personal troops, so when uprisings had happened everywhere, they hadn't been able to cope with all of it.

"All right. I'll tell the king I'm ready to take his sister as my wife."

"Sure, as you should. But for today…" Seraphina moved in closer. "I want you to make love to me. I had to wait so long during your campaign for the capital."

I hugged Seraphina very, very tightly.

"I won't lose to some girl."

"I know. I don't expect my love for you to fade, either."

When I told him I was ready to accept his proposal, Hasse was even more pleased than I'd expected. He then said he'd arrange a meeting between me and his sister, Lumie. Speaking of, I didn't remember ever meeting a girl called Lumie, the reason being that she'd been put into a convent. If Hasse had failed to obtain the crown, he'd intended to just have her be a nun.

To be fair, being with Hasse might put her life in danger. The longer she spent studying at the convent, the safer she was. In any case, she was quite far back in the line of succession, so leaving her there wasn't an issue.

Of course, my wife-to-be was young enough to be called a child, so the marriage would be something of a formality. King Hasse wanted to make his regent into one of his relatives.

She may have been put in a convent, but she was unmistakably royal. I was a bit worried she'd be proud and horribly arrogant. If she complained about me to her brother, Hasse, it could make me look bad, too.

Taking a seat in the meeting room, I waited for her to come. Guards stood outside, but inside the room would be just the two of us.

However, even as the arranged time came, Lumie didn't appear.

Weird… Is she late on purpose, trying to show she's above me?

——Hey, Alsrod, I can feel someone's presence. Someone else is here in the room. I'm sure of it.

Apparently, Oda Nobunaga could sense people's presences. What a cool profession.

It can't be an assassin, can it? I put a hand on my sword. I was good enough to take them if it was one or two.

——No, they clearly don't mean to kill you.

The window was closed, yet I thought I noticed the curtains swaying unnaturally.

"Is someone behind that curtain?" I asked carefully, trying not to scare them.

After I called out, a young girl with her hair neatly tied up peeked her face out from the curtain.

"Oh dear, you finally caught me!" Smiling broadly, she walked briskly up to me and bowed her head. "How do you do, Your Excellency? I am Lumie, the new king's sister."

She at least didn't seem to be afraid of me.

I stood up from my seat and greeted her. "Pleased to meet you. I am Alsrod Nayvil, Marquess of Fordoneria, now serving as regent."

"Wow… You are quite a tall gentleman," she gushed, as if she'd seen a rare animal. Lumie stood up on tiptoe and tried measuring her height against mine. I was over a head taller, by the way.

"I don't think I'm especially tall for a man. Maybe you're just small, Princess."

"I also thought all gentlemen grew beards, but not you, I see. In fact, your chin is smooth and clean."

"Yes, beard hair bothers me, so I shave it off."

This girl says strange things, I thought, a bit amused.

"I hardly ever got to meet any gentlemen in the convent, so I was frightened. That's why I was watching from behind the curtain. I was going to try to run if you were like an orc or an ogre."

"Don't worry; they only live in the Northlands or on the frontier."

I could tell right away from our conversation that she was really sheltered—very befitting of a princess indeed.

"Besides, I heard you've proven yourself in many battles in the past, so I thought maybe you were quite a barbaric man."

I laughed out loud. She was such an honest girl.

"I will not deny being barbaric. I have even killed people on many occasions. In your convent's teachings, I might be a terrific scoundrel."

"Not at all." She shook her head. "You know, I can tell if someone is a scoundrel or not by looking in their eyes. You have bright eyes. So you're a good person."

"Perhaps they only look so because I kill without remorse, not because I'm a good person," I said, deliberately testing her.

"Don't worry. I can tell by the way they shine that you're not a bad man. So you pass." Lumie suddenly came over and hugged me tightly.

"You might be rather frightening, but you're not a bad person. I'll be your wife. I can't wait."

"What if I'm secretly a monster in disguise?"

© Kaito Shibano

"I've been serving the gods for all this time, so I don't think they would let me marry one."

Her logic was rather full of holes, but since she said it with so much conviction, I felt like I was going crazy myself.

It was more like I'd gained a sister than a wife. Play-marriage might not be so bad, either.

"Oh, Your Excellency, I have a question."

"Yes, what is it?"

"Do you really intend to usurp this kingdom from my brother?"

What a horrific question to be asked point-blank.

"I've heard news of what is happening in the country from the convent, and I just couldn't dismiss that feeling. Even the nuns were saying the same…"

"My thoughts are concentrated solely on defeating the king's enemies."

Lumie hugged me again, smiling from ear to ear.

"Thank you so much!"

There I was, lying to my wife-to-be the moment I met her; I probably really was a bad man.

Afterward, I introduced Lumie to Seraphina. Lumie fearlessly showered her with questions, too, leaving Seraphina at a loss.

Honestly, I'd never seen Seraphina so overwhelmed by someone else, so it was a bit refreshing for me as an onlooker. I was sure it was distressing for her, of course.

Seraphina complained to me about it when we were alone.

"I knew she was young, but I didn't think she'd be like that…"

"Yeah. She's so innocent it's hard to know how to respond to her."

"She just seems like a little sister to me."

"Funny, I thought the same thing. She's a totally different type than Altia, though."

Seraphina sighed quietly. "You have to marry that girl, darling. But it might not be easy."

"Teach her what you can for me. I can't really spare the time."

My workload had exploded since we'd taken the capital. A regent really did have to do everything himself. My tasks were virtually endless. The situation in the surrounding area hadn't exactly calmed down, so I didn't have the time to rejoice over this marriage.

"All right," Seraphina replied. "But…even if she hasn't taken the vows, she's still an innocent little convent girl. I'd feel guilty telling her about the wedding night."

"That sort of thing…can wait till much later…" I didn't feel comfortable talking about that so openly, even if we were alone. "But I don't think she's too young to get married, either."

I mean, even girls under ten got handed off in political marriages sometimes. Even seven- and eight-year-olds had gotten married in the royal family's history. But marriage itself was a separate matter from... everything else.

"My, look who's getting all flustered!"

"I was hoping you wouldn't notice."

"I suppose it is reassuring, though." Seraphina moved closer to me. "I'll let her be your official wife, but remember I'm the one who cares about you the most, darling..." Her eyes looked a bit troubled. "If I could have my way, I wouldn't let anyone else have you. Not Miss Laviala, not Fleur, not any other woman. But I'm too good to complain about such things."

"I know that better than anyone in the world. You really are clever."

Seraphina could keep political decisions separate from her feelings. That said, she couldn't be happy about getting demoted.

"So to keep me from getting upset at times like this, make sure you love me."

To help reassure her, I drew Seraphina to my chest and ran my fingers through her black hair.

I asked Laviala and Kelara to tell me the most important thing I should do as regent. Both of them had been given land and honorary titles around the same time I became regent.

"I think human resource development," Laviala said.

"You have more land to manage now. There is a limit to setting up advisers as magistrates or governors," added Kelara. "I think perhaps you should try to find new people you can use."

Their two opinions were mostly the same. I'd already asked Kelara beforehand, so I pretty much knew her answer, but it seemed Laviala had a similar view.

"Right. I'll promote more and more of our best people. Of course, formally they'll be serving the royal family, but still."

A regent was ultimately an assistant to the king. Blatantly dominating the royal family's jurisdiction from day one wouldn't be very kosher.

"May I offer a suggestion?" Kelara spoke up. "In regard to governing the cities, I think if you used those cities' merchants as bureaucrats, their knowledge of the land would make things more efficient. Of course, there's a risk they might only say what benefits the merchants."

"True. If there's anyone good at finance like Fanneria, I'd like to use them. I still need soldiers, too, but they'd be useless if they didn't do things how I want anyway." I was confident my troops were the most disciplined in all the country by now. However, it wasn't possible to control the whole kingdom with their current numbers. Even if I could get enough recruits, the extra riffraff would cause the quality to suffer if I did nothing else. I'd need to turn them into proper soldiers. "I still need the bureaucrats regardless."

This time Laviala was the one to raise her hand. Though for some reason, she flashed a glare at Kelara. Was there some kind of rivalry here...?

"Perhaps you could use a priest? Men of the cloth are quite knowledgeable as well."

"Makes sense. That's not a bad idea." First a person had to be literate to be good at managing money and negotiating. Priests already had that bar cleared, but... "Temples have different sects, too, though... It'd be dangerous if we didn't manage them well..."

——**Well, why don't you try giving a *kakyo*?**

Oda Nobunaga said something strange.
What's a kakyo*? I have no idea what you're talking about.*

——**Put simply, it's a paper test. You promote the ones who complete it with good scores. Not that I've ever done it myself; it was a method used in a country across the sea. If it works out, you might**

be able to create a bureaucracy directly tied to you. I can't guarantee it'll work out, of course.

Huh, that might be interesting.

If it was just test scores, it had nothing to do with personal connections. I'd be able to tell who was actually the most capable, or at least who was good at taking tests. Besides, I might be able to get some good ideas by making the last question something like "What is a policy you would suggest?"

"Both of you—I have an idea." My profession's ideas were basically my own. "We'll hold a test in the capital and choose a portion of the bureaucrats based on the results. Anyone can participate if they like. The questions will cover famous scriptures and finance. Maybe we can test geography and history knowledge and even familiarity with the classics while we're at it."

"Huh…? A test…?! That sounds just like university…" Laviala's jaw dropped.

Maybe it was. Such a test was unheard of anywhere else, at least. Certainly not for officials.

"It's a rather unusual method… With no precedent, it's hard to say…" Kelara seemed to be confused by something so unorthodox. I was going to be creating a new political system regardless.

"I'm doing it. The nobility are just there by inheritance, so I can't trust them as bureaucrats anyway, but if I find that any of them are exceptionally smart, I can still use them."

Thus, by my will alone, the civil service examination was born.

I was told there was quite a stir when the civil service examination was announced on town bulletin boards. It was an unusual idea, that anyone could become a bureaucrat if they scored well on a test. Naturally, people of low birth didn't have as many educational opportunities, so it would be difficult for them to qualify. But perhaps priests or others in a similar situation could still become bureaucrats if they were smart, even though they were lower class.

On the other hand, there were complaints from petty landowners on the capital outskirts, who'd mostly inherited their positions as bureaucrats or other types of professionals.

I responded to their complaints as follows: "If you score well on the examination, I will have no problem hiring you. I look forward to your success."

It was hard to keep quality personnel with hereditary succession alone. A total meritocracy would present its own challenges, but the right amount of social mobility should energize a society.

Actually, my own vassals were a medley from different areas. I had almost none of the Nayvil clan's longest-serving vassals, and with good reason—because there weren't many vassals in the Nayvils' tiny original territory to begin with. My territory had exploded in size, so I had no choice but to absorb lots of different people.

"Do you really think this is going to work out…?" the new king, Hasse, asked me anxiously. He didn't want me doing anything too peculiar; that much I could sympathize with.

"Your Majesty, the capital's kings have been driven out time and time again. The reason is that they were too dependent on the existing system. They fell to their enemies because that system was defective."

"I see… You may be right…"

"Therefore, we first need to sift out and find the most capable people. In extreme terms, the lowlifes who talk behind your back but are good at their jobs would serve you much better than the lowlifes who merely claim to be loyal."

"To think of using someone who might stab you in the back at any—"

"If everyone serving you were sincere about their loyalty, I think they would have come to your side when you lived in seclusion."

Hasse fell silent.

That was his answer. Most lords, after all, had abandoned the royal family. They didn't dare to finish the family off, but they still didn't have any real intention of siding with those who'd fallen.

"I shall make the capital area flourish—of that you can be certain. That is the real way to keep the former king's forces from growing." I always made sure to remind Hasse that everything I did was for him.

"Very well. Also, about the wedding plans…"

"Yes, that is proceeding smoothly as well."

Lumie's teachers were fellow women: Kelara for academics, Seraphina for general tutelage. Lumie showed her face occasionally, but she seemed to be quite dedicated to her studies.

There was one such time when she was reading intently through an old text.

"Your Excellency, I want some books from the classics, but they seem rather few and far between. Would you know of any?"

That was a fairly specialized question. I'd never read any such books myself.

"Princess Lumie is truly outstanding. She received a very good foundation at the convent." Kelara seemed rather impressed, for her part.

"Princess Lumie takes everything to heart, so she picks it up quickly," Seraphina agreed, seated next to me. "She's still a bit naive, but I'll take care of that. I'll make her a wife you can be proud of, darling."

"All right. I'll look forward to it."

Seraphina truly never disappointed me.

Three months passed.

Lumie and I had our wedding ceremony. As it was a wedding between the king's sister and his regent, lords and priests visited from throughout the kingdom. The rural lords, in particular, might've feared being branded as enemies if they didn't come to celebrate.

Before the ceremony, I met again with Lumie, now all dressed up.

"Ah, Your Excellency. Or rather, maybe from today I should call you *dear*."

All the flowers in the palace garden would be ashamed to show their faces at the sight of the beautiful young girl who stood before me. With her tiara full of jewels, she was adorned in luxury—but nothing about her was over-the-top; it was all very tasteful.

"That's odd. I thought you were someone a bit more childish; I can hardly believe you have become such a fine young lady."

"I learned so much from Lady Seraphina and Miss Kelara. Any refinement I might possess is all thanks to their effort." Lumie beamed.

"I'm in trouble now. If you're this beautiful, I'll earn the envy of the king's other vassals."

"You flatter me, sir. I made every effort to be good enough for you. I'm the one who is so shamefully uneducated."

Seraphina was smiling behind her, as if to ask, *How is she? I did a good job, didn't I?*

My influence in the capital is this much greater now. More than anything, though, I honestly just want to thank the gods that I get to marry such a gorgeous girl.

——You could thank me, too. If not for me, you might've stayed a petty lord's little brother.

Must you interrupt right now? But yes, I know, I'm grateful to you, too.
Maybe it was a bit odd for me to thank the gods, though.

"Well, shall we go, Lumie?" I took her hand.

"Yes, dear. I'll be a good wife."

I walked slowly toward the officiating priest.

In a formal wedding, the couple was supposed to exchange a kiss, and so the priest told us to do so.

"I'm so happy, dear."

"I promise to make you happy. This kiss is my vow."

The instant we kissed, I was bound to the royal family by marriage. I was one step closer to the power and influence of a king.

◇

A great many more participants appeared for the civil service exam than I'd planned on.

I dispatched scholars to serve as proctors at the test site; there was always the chance that we might have some cheaters among the exam takers. Tests to become a scholar were already being given in the capital, so our exam's format was based on that format. However, with the number of examinees literally an order of magnitude more than expected, we had to add more test sites.

The day of the test, I inspected the sites together with Kelara and Laviala. There was a kid balancing his pen on his nose as he thought, and even a raggedy old man who looked like some kind of freewheeling sage.

"They all seem to be struggling," Laviala commented.

"These are the exam questions, by the way. Think you can solve them, Laviala?" I asked.

Laviala immediately looked stumped. "I don't know any of these…"

"Good thing you started out as my vassal. You would've had a hard time getting hired." Of course, when Laviala showed off her prowess with the bow, I probably would've hired her for that anyway.

"Would anybody know the answers to these, Miss Kelara?" Laviala asked, sighing.

Her expression indifferent, Kelara took the question sheet Laviala offered. "My memory is hazy for a few parts, but I think I could probably answer seventy percent." Kelara never tried to brag, so 70 percent was probably her honest opinion.

"Seventy percent… You're a genius…," Laviala said despondently. "Lord Alsrod, you're going to be disappointed in me now…"

"No, I'm not. Quit your worrying. Some of my guard troops can't even read properly. There's a job fit for everyone."

"That's right. Besides, Miss Laviala, you're quite sharp yourself. This was just what I was always taught, so it's my strong suit."

Vassals close to the royal family were required to be cultured, after all. If someone really crude were serving the king, the king's dignity itself would come into question.

"I suppose that's reassuring. Still, I wonder how many people could actually solve problems as hard as these? I can't imagine one or two thousand people being able to do it."

"I don't need two thousand new officials, so it's fine. Fifty would be outstanding for this first round."

When completely uneducated people became bureaucrats, it often caused conflict with the people being governed. Having some fundamental knowledge also made the work go more smoothly from the first day.

"Quite true. Besides, the merchant class is quite well off recently, so more people are studying things like the classics now, rather than just economics. Many are sending their children to university, too."

"Things are so much easier when you always know what I mean, Kelara." She was right. Now I would pick out the qualified people from the classes who were previously far removed from the bureaucracy, and I would put them under my control—well, technically under the king's control. "A country can't be governed with just soldiers, after all. You absolutely need a bureaucrat class. This will be the first step in creating that class. Otherwise, it'll be a problem when it's time for realm-building."

My voice got just a little stronger when I said the word *realm-building*. Someday I'd build a realm where I was leader. In fact, if I didn't go that far, I wouldn't have a future. At the very least, the Nayvil clan wouldn't have a future.

Even in the past, lords who hadn't fully secured their authority had disappeared after getting assassinated or falling to rebels. Growing too powerful had made them lots of enemies.

On the other hand, even if the dynasty in my time had to borrow the strength of military cliques or powerful lords, it had survived for a long time. That was because the first king had worked without rest to lay down clear foundations for the kingdom.

If I stayed regent, I'd eventually lose to someone who tried to overthrow me. And even if no problems arose while I was alive, who knew about my heir?

——Good thinking. Even in my world, sometimes there were sudden rebellions after succession. It's a time of vulnerability, after all. When Qin Shi Huang died, his realm ceased to function. Even the Taira clan might've been able to keep fighting a bit longer if Kiyomori had lived another ten years.

You still insist on using words I don't understand, but I definitely know what you mean.

My kids were still young, but I might as well try to leave things in a stable condition for them.

"Lord Alsrod, you have an especially faraway look today," Laviala pointed out. "You look like you're thinking about things decades away."

"That's because I was, actually."

Laviala let out a carefree "Wow…" and said, "It's pretty hard being a regent, huh?"

I'd still be thinking this much if I weren't regent, though. Whether it was realistic or not, all lords thought about it at some point—how much they'd like to create their own realm. Since I had the chance now, I'd have to put it to good use.

The test results were out two days later.

Out of about 850 people, thirty-eight scored over 70 percent. That was a perfect number for now. For a second test, I had them interviewed.

As regent, I at least showed up for all the interviews. I also called in people like Kelara and my financial officer, Fanneria, to cover what I didn't know.

"What do you think should be done to make the realm prosperous? You won't be punished for anything you say, so answer as you will." I wanted to ask something abstract.

- **Expand the economy.**
- **Increase farmland by developing uncultivated lands.**
- **Reduce military spending by quickly ending the war.**

I got quite a variety of answers, but I decided to pass those who could clearly state their opinions, regardless of validity. Among them was someone who answered, "You can win the war by using the weapon I have created. It is also good for hunting."

He was a middle-aged man with a beard and fiery eyes. He looked more like an engineer than a scholar. Someone inventing a new siege weapon wouldn't be too surprising.

I double-checked his name—Ortonba. *That's a strange name*, I thought and then realized, *Oh, he's a dwarf.* He was quite short, after all. A lot of dwarves were short, even as adults. Kelara was quite tall, though, perhaps because she had a more varied ancestry.

"What sort of weapon would that be?" I asked him.

"Sir, it is called a gun or a firearm. Using the power of gunpowder, it hurls a small ball out of a metal tube, striking the enemy."

"How is it different from a bow?"

"Completely different, sir. It is mostly unaffected by wind and extremely deadly. I believe it would take far less time to train someone compared with the bow as well. However, it won't ignite when wet, so it is less effective in rain."

Fanneria's wolf ears twitched. Perhaps his merchant senses had picked up the scent of profit. "My name is Fanneria. This weapon—why did you decide to create it?"

"The dwarf village where I live is often raided by bandits. We can usually drive them off, but it is difficult for just the menfolk to keep watch at night. Thus, I wondered if I could create a weapon that could be wielded even by womenfolk and children," Ortonba explained. "I am a smith by trade, and in my village I've long employed gunpowder for warnings or attacks. Gunpowder is efficient for mountain work, you see. So then I wondered if I couldn't do something with this."

I was curious now myself.

"It didn't go well at all at first. I even almost died from an explosion. It would seem my profession is quite well suited to this, however, as the development has made great progress."

The word *profession* didn't escape my notice. "Wait. Just what is your profession?"

"Yes, it's quite a unique one, so you may not believe me, but...it's called Kunitomo Shuu. It appears to be related to smithery."

——Did he say Kunitomo Shuu?!

The conqueror in my mind was shouting.

Hey, you know something about this, Nobunaga?

——Kunitomo was the land of gunsmiths. Essentially, it was where guns were made.

So you had these "guns" in your world, too. Were they powerful?

——You could say that. I once annihilated an entire cavalry regiment with them. Cavalry can't fight without getting in close. So I destroyed them piecemeal using guns. Even armor didn't save them. I killed several of their generals, too.

You should've told me about this before... Come on...

——Even if I told you, I don't know enough to teach you how to make them. It'd be impossible to convey everything verbally anyway. It's not like assembling a ladder, you know.

I guess that's true. If somebody told me to make a sword on my own, I don't know that I could.

"All right. Ortonba, you're hired. However, I'm more interested in these guns than in making you a bureaucrat. Show us what you know."

"Most certainly. Now, perhaps this is a strange request to make right away, but might I be able to get a more respectable person as tax collector for my village...? He is a rather unscrupulous character; every time he comes to collect taxes, he always demands we have a feast, which is a burden not unlike another tax for us..."

"Agreed. If you do a good-enough job, I'll even halve your village's tax. Next time, bring me this 'firearm.'"

After Ortonba left, I couldn't stop grinning. "With such a massive population, it's no wonder the capital has some unusual professions."

"Indeed, my Akechi Mitsuhide profession is quite unusual, too, so I felt a sort of kinship with him." Kelara looked totally serious, but only because she still had her "work face" on.

The interviews were divided over a few days, so after the next day's interviews concluded, I brought Ortonba back again. What he held was indeed a metal tube. He said he wanted us to set up archery targets, so I promptly took him to the outdoor archery range.

"We have nice sunny weather today, so I believe this should go quite well."

"Right. Show me what this thing can do."

I had him stand at the same distance a normal archer would. Ortonba said he could hit it from farther away, but using the same setup as for bows would make it easier to tell the difference.

"I am only a smith, so my aim is not the best, but...nevertheless, at this distance, it is impossible to miss." Lighting the cord on the back, Ortonba pointed the tube at the target. "Ah right, right— There'll be a loud noise, so you may want to plug your—"

Baaaaang!

Before he was done speaking, there was an ear-piercing crack. The noise reverberated as a strange ringing deep within my ears. The sound was so loud that temple-goers might mistake it for some sort of devilry. A few people even fell over in fright.

What was really important, though, was its results. On the edge of the target was a hole as big as my thumb. When a soldier went to check, a pointed ball was stuck in the hard earth behind it.

"What do you think? It can easily deliver a mortal wound at even twice this distance. You can even try it against armor, if you want. If it's not exceedingly thick, it'll go right through."

"Ortonba, from this year on, your village can just pay half its tax," I declared right then and there.

If I got my hands on this weapon, it was a bargain.

$\diamond$

I ordered Ortonba to manufacture and improve his firearms. I'd asked him to improve them because Oda Nobunaga had offered an idea.

——These are without a doubt authentic firearms, but their efficiency could use some work. When the match cord and bullet are separate like this, it makes for one more step in the process.

If you're going to mention it, tell me everything, I thought, but this job of mine was always stingy.

——Let that dwarf creature think about the rest. I'm not exactly well acquainted with all the details of the process myself, you know. Besides, this world has another concept you call magic.

Eh, complaining too much was getting annoying, so I'd leave things there. There weren't any problems with the guns as they were for now anyway.

And then, once the talk about Ortonba was finished, I got a message in my mind:

Special ability Conqueror's Insight leveled up! In addition to your city- and trade-related economic sense being like Oda Nobunaga's, you can identify people who have outstanding skills. As long as you are not intoxicated and your mind is not otherwise clouded, it is always active.

That's nice, but it would've been even nicer to have this before the interviews. Then I would've known immediately who had the right talent.

——You're confused about what should happen when. I'm retroactively acknowledging that you showed you have what it takes to acquire this. If you'd lived your life doing nothing, you wouldn't have gotten any new abilities even with me as your profession.

I see—so you mean I have to gain experience to improve.

Admittedly, if people got these crazy abilities just by receiving a profession, the history books would look ridiculous. It'd be a real hassle if every few years some peasant with hero potential showed up and caused a rebellion.

Anyway, now I shouldn't overlook anyone's unusual talents. It was easy enough to spot those of high-ranking people, but there might be geniuses hiding among the commoners—diamonds in the rough. In particular, by giving tests like I just had, I might be able to hire people of low standing. If there were some high achievers mixed in who could overturn the values of the nobility, I definitely wanted to find them.

And so we continued with the next interviews.

Since I'd narrowed down the field quite a bit with the first test, trying to pick the top talent out of the current pool was actually harder. These candidates must've had some brains if they were still in the running, after all.

And then, there came the third person that day.

"My name is Yanhaan Grantrix," a dragonewt woman said in a leisurely rhythm. Just like that, the atmosphere turned somehow serene.

"Holding an exam in the capital really does attract a variety of different races. I've heard dragonewts come from the lands far out west, but I seem to recall you're not even originally from this continent?"

"Yes. I came to this land seventy-six years ago and began trading in medicines. I expanded my business to the capital, and now I run six stores on the continent."

She looked like she was still in her twenties, but they did say dragonewts were long-lived like elves, so that probably explained her youthful appearance.

"Since you passed the test, you must know a lot about old customs. So why did you want to be a bureaucrat?"

"Weeell, I wanted to try something new during my long life." She was very laid-back, almost like this wasn't an interview, but she must've been quite a good saleswoman. I wasn't going to be fooled by appearances. "Alsooo, I want to spread my tea philosophy."

"'Tea philosophy'?" *This woman says some strange things*, I thought. But then, Yanhaan Grantrix's eyes—I couldn't even tell where they were looking—opened wide. Dragonewts had big pupils, and I could sense something like confidence and determination behind them.

My body jerked suddenly.

Special ability Conqueror's Insight has discovered a rare talent!
Type: Special technical skill

Interesting— *So this ability strengthens my own intuition.*

"Isn't tea something you chat with friends and colleagues over? You put out some snacks, relax, and talk after lunch or after supper."

"I think that sort of tea is nice, too. Howeeeever, there is no soul in it. It is merely idle chatter."

My financial officer, Fanneria, looked a bit annoyed, which was rare for him. "I must say I am most displeased by your attempts to blow smoke in His Excellency's face."

They didn't seem to be compatible, even though they were both merchants.

"I have no such intentions. I am perfectly serious. Tea provides a person the time to quiet their mind and confront their inner selves."

"In that case, I would like you to be more specific. If you're a merchant yourself, you should stop talking about the soul and other such ill-defined ideas."

So from Fanneria's perspective, people who spoke of ambiguities couldn't be trusted. And it was hard to work with someone you couldn't trust, after all.

"Talking about that would be impossible," replied Yanhaan. "For the soul is not something that can be described in words."

Fanneria's wolflike ears stood straight up, and he seemed annoyed. "Your Excellency, this merchant is highly suspicious. I think it would be best not to trust someone like her."

"Now, now, just hold on." I held my hand up to Fanneria. "Yanhaan, were you given some kind of unusual profession?"

"You are very perceptive." Yanhaan returned to her relaxed vibe. "I came over from another continent, so I received my profession much longer after coming of age; in fact, it was just twenty years ago."

I guess she was already an adult, then?

"I still don't quite understand it myself, but my profession is Sen no Rikyuu. I wonder what language it's from?"

Yanhaan didn't look like she was feigning ignorance. I didn't know what kind of profession that was, either, but I figured it was similar to what Kelara and I had.

——Haaa-ha-ha-ha-ha-ha! I see, so there's even a Rikyuu! I think I've figured out this world's "professions."

So you recognize the name?

——It seems the people from my time period function as professions in this world. I don't know how it works, but there hasn't been a Kuukai or Prince Shoutoku, so that must be it. This might mean Monkey, Shingen, and many others could show up, too.

Monkey was a bizarre profession name; what the hell was that about? Maybe his world had some sort of monkey god.

"Just out of curiosity, has this Sen no Rikyuu ever spoken to you inside your mind?"

"I've never had that happen. Buuut, for some reason I do feel like this mysterious profession talks to me. 'Go. Tell the world about tea,' it says."

Fanneria scowled once again at the vagueness. Kelara, on the other hand, remained expressionless as she listened, so I wasn't quite sure how she felt.

"Very well," I said. "I'd like you to teach me about the soul of tea, as you call it. What do we need to prepare?"

"I will show you, if you come to my residence in your everyday clothes. Though, I suppose for a regent like you that would still be quite fancy."

"Er...Your Excellency, this could be a surprise attack. I cannot quite recommend going—"

"Fanneria, I know a thing or two about swords. Besides, Laviala will protect me if I have her there, too."

You couldn't discount an idea before you tried it anyway.

Before the arranged day, I had the rappas investigate Yanhaan and the tea she was trying to popularize. I'd increased my number of rappas, so I could assign them to these sorts of tasks as well. The ones I used in the cities were more of an auxiliary force that didn't have a ton of military training, however.

Yadoriggy came all the way up to my second-story bedroom to make her report. When I left the window open, she could make her way in from along the wall.

"You're a servant today, huh?" I said.

She was dressed like one of the maids who worked in the castle. Her wolf ears were conspicuous, but there were other werewolf maids, so it wasn't too unusual. Still, I would hate to deal with a servant with eyes this wicked.

Yadoriggy gave no answer. "Speak," I told her, realizing I hadn't given her permission yet. If she were ever captured, she'd probably keep her mouth shut until she died if I didn't give the order as her master.

"Looking weak or of low position is one of the basics. If your opponent looks down on you, you can take advantage," Yadoriggy explained, all while kneeling with head bowed.

"I don't mind that line of thinking. Well, did you find anything out? And you can raise your head. You spies are so particular about everything, even manners."

With a quick "As you wish," Yadoriggy sat on the bed. From there, she had a good view of the room. She must've wanted a good spot for dealing with any intruders. "Yanhaan has held many tea parties she calls 'tea ceremonies.' Because of her position, it seems to have become quite popular among merchants. Even many of the former king's bureaucrats have joined in."

"So it really is a social event, then." In that case, it wasn't too different from any other tea party.

"It's actually an extremely ceremonial affair, where the host and a guest enjoy tea across from each other in an extraordinarily small room. The room is a strange thing in itself, seemingly made just for the purpose of tea ceremony."

"Huh. Yanhaan did mention some religious ideas."

"Speaking of, it seems you don't believe in religion yourself, Your Excellency?" Yadoriggy uncharacteristically asked me a question of her own accord.

"I can't say for certain, but I think my profession's power will weaken if I devote myself to a particular faith."

"Yes, sir. However, there is a risk Orsent Cathedral may turn against you if they find out you don't support them, so please be aware of that."

Orsent Cathedral was the de facto ruler of Fortwest Prefecture and arguably the greatest power in the capital area.

"I'll keep that in mind. Also, how are the background checks for the preexisting bureaucrats coming along?"

"Quite well," Yadoriggy answered, nodding. "As we thought, there seem to be some number still on the former king's side."

Having a list of people with connections to the previous king was highly convenient. That said, some of them were probably only trying to play both sides, rather than actually counting themselves among the former king's faction.

"Well, as for Yanhaan's tea ceremony, I won't know the truth if I don't show up. That's all I had to discuss for today, but..." A sudden urge came over me, and I gave in. I went closer and placed a hand on Yadoriggy's shoulder. "Are the rappas well versed in the ways of pleasing a man?"

"Surely there must be plenty of ladies more beautiful than I."

Yadoriggy's total indifference just made me want her even more.

"If you don't see yourself as beautiful, you don't know much about yourself."

"Then I am in your hands. What is your desire?"

"Well, this is hard to say, but there are some things I can't ask Seraphina or Laviala to do."

Yadoriggy gave a small nod. "I don't mind, but since I'm always so stoic, you might be disappointed."

"You never know until you try." I removed Yadoriggy's maid outfit. Her naked body was so covered in scars I wondered if touching her would hurt her. "I feel like a doctor. Or maybe a torturer."

"They're all shallow wounds. I have to force my way through narrow spaces, so these are mostly cuts from that. Although I was tortured once when someone thought I was suspicious."

Just as she'd said, Yadoriggy remained stoic even as I touched her, and she began to caress me halfway through. I could tell right away this woman had led a completely different life from my wives.

Once we had finished, Yadoriggy stoically asked, "How was it?" Her lithe body sat upon the bed. She was so slender I wondered how she could handle the rappas' violent missions.

"You know," I replied, "being a woman's plaything is pretty nice."

I was fully alert with the night breeze coming in. Since I couldn't sleep anyway, I might as well take care of one more bit of business.

Soon I had my first big undertaking since becoming regent. Tea ceremony would be my diversion before that.

◇

I took Laviala with me to the tea ceremony, along with a few other military officers from my top vassals. Also, since Kelara had apparently experienced tea ceremony back when she lived in the capital, she already knew what she was doing when we entered Yanhaan's residence. It would've been nice if she'd mentioned that to begin with.

Yanhaan was already waiting in the ceremony room, where we were apparently meant to go in one by one. When I tried to enter, her servant explained to me, "Swords, knives, and all other weapons and armor must be set aside before entering, as per custom."

"It's too dangerous for you to go in there unarmed—you haven't even hired this person yet!" Laviala complained behind me. That was what she needed to say, as that was her job. This woman was like both a wife and a sister to me. And that would never change. Whether I was going to listen to what she said was another story, though.

"I'm going to do as I'm told," I replied. "Besides, I'm sure Yanhaan doesn't want to lose her life, either."

Many people serving me had come to the residence as well. If I died, not a soul in Yanhaan's family would survive. Naturally, I'd had the rappas conduct a basic background check on her as well. There was no sign that Yanhaan had connections to the former king.

"Very well... But please run away at the first sign of danger..."

"I'm happy to see you're as loyal as always."

"You always did have a tendency to rush into things on your own," Laviala replied, blushing; maybe my compliment had caught her off guard.

"I won't deny that, but you're not so different yourself. You would've been killed if I hadn't saved you that one time."

"Well...I was only doing my duty as a vassal. It wasn't a big deal," Laviala said, clearly thinking only of her own situation.

Anyway, time to see what this tea ceremony's all about.

I was bewildered upon opening the small door. The room itself was tiny, only about the width of the door. It didn't go back very far, either. Not even jails were this cramped.

In the center of the room was a table connected to the wall that took up much of what space there was. You couldn't really get to the other side without going under it. On either side of the table was a chair; Yanhaan was sitting on the far end. When we first met, she was very genial and warm; but now, she had a sort of strength you'd expect from a master of an art form.

"Welcome. It is a pleasure to have you. Please, do have a seat."

A tea set was upon the table. Since this was called tea ceremony, it must involve drinking tea. I sat down in the seat offered to me.

"What a strange room. It might even be the perfect size for a confessional. Sitting to drink tea is about all you can do otherwise."

"Yes, that's exactly right. In tea ceremony one uses tea to temper the soul, so having too many things on hand would simply get in the way."

Yanhaan poured what was presumably tea into a cup from the teapot. This drink had a disturbingly green color to it, however. It was completely unlike the amber color of any tea I'd seen.

"What on earth is this? It looks just like poison..."

"If it seems suspicious, perhaps I should drink first?"

"No, it's fine. Taking an antidote first should be good enough."

——Tea ceremony, eh? Never would've imagined anyone in this world serving green-colored tea.

Judging by Oda Nobunaga's reaction, I could trust her. I put the tea in my mouth. True to its color, it had a unique flavor—bitter, but also sweet. I wouldn't call it unpleasant, either.

"Please quiet your mind as you taste the tea. It is a recipe made just for this ceremony."

Doing as my host bid, I drank the strange-tasting tea.

To my shock, I realized I could no longer hear anything.

My mind really did become quiet. However, even though I'd merely drunk tea, for some reason I felt like I was almost meditating, as if at a temple. This "tea ceremony" might be perfect to do before making big political decisions. It sure did influence the mind. This was unlike any tea party I was familiar with.

I suddenly felt like something was pulling me in... No, was I really getting pulled in? It was a bizarre sensation, as if I were falling into myself.

Maybe I really was pois—

◇

When I came to, I was lying in a strange place. Strange was the only way to describe it. I was unsure if the pure-white ground was floor or earth, and above it hung an endless fog.

"Whoa, whoa— If this is the afterlife, I'm not laughing."

Maybe I'd gotten complacent after becoming regent. Laviala and my other officers would probably avenge me, but with my children so young, the realm would fall into disarray once again.

"It's not the afterlife, so feel free to laugh."

I turned around at the voice behind me. There stood a strange man who seemed familiar, though this was our first meeting. His appearance was so similar to mine it was like I was looking at myself. His hair was black, but otherwise he was not much different from myself. I wasn't sure of his age. He looked both far older than me and the same age. I couldn't figure out what country's clothes he was wearing, but they were boldly decorated. He must've been pretty high ranking.

"Who the hell are you? And where the hell is this?" I asked as I stood up.

"Such insolence. But I suppose I can't be too upset; you've always been that way." The man looked truly amused. "It is I, the conqueror Oda Nobunaga. And I am your profession, Alsrod." For someone making such an forceful statement, he was being incredibly forthright. "Tea has the effect of making people extremely introspective, you see. You must have fallen too deep inside yourself. Even Rikyuu's tea never had that great an effect, however. Was it drugged? Or perhaps this land's tea is different from the Land of the Rising Sun's?"

Oda Nobunaga kept on saying the most incredible things so nonchalantly. The dragonewt Yanhaan was indeed a seller of medicine, so maybe she had laced my drink with some kind of drug. It hadn't tasted like it was drugged, though. Because of my position, I'd deliberately eaten things that tasted like poison in order to recognize the flavors.

"You expect me to believe you so quickly? To be fair, though, I can't think of any other explanation for where this is or who you are. Blaming it on the tea does make sense. It's far more likely to be the cause than what I had for dinner last night, at least."

The man grinned in a very disarming sort of way. "Just as I'd expect from someone with me as their profession. You're very quick."

"I bet no one in the world thought they'd ever come face-to-face with their profession." I took another good look at this Oda Nobunaga man. He had a severe look about him—completely unlike me—yet there was something of me there. There was no way I could be related to someone out of this world, though, so it must've been a total coincidence.

"It's not exactly impossible, now is it?" said Oda Nobunaga. "In this world you receive your professions from the gods. And this land's priests—regardless of whether it's true or not—have conversations with the gods."

"So you're saying we should be able to talk with the professions those gods bestow? Professions don't have any personalities. Fighter, Monk, Merchant—they're all just profession names, not some person's name."

"Generally, yes. But there are others besides you with professions that are obviously a person's name, like Mitsuhide or Rikyuu. They may be the exception, but Alsrod, you too are exceptional. If professions don't have personalities, just who have you been speaking to all this time? Is it just a delusion of yours?"

"True. It wouldn't make sense to be skeptical at this point." I'd always been one for embracing risks and unknowns. I decided to fully accept things as they were.

"You're just like me, though, Alsrod. You have striking eyes."

"Was that compliment intended for me or yourself? Well, the Nayvil clan did have a lot of good-looking people, they say."

"I'm not concerned with your bloodline. I mean something deeper down. Your face has the look of a man who wants it all. I never saw anyone with that look in Japan. I was the only one."

I was actually starting to enjoy this myself. I could really get along with this man.

"Naturally. I'm not stopping at regent. Someday I'll form my own realm. I'm sure it'll take time, of course. I don't have the justification yet, and the people don't want a new dynasty, either."

Forming a dynasty while ignoring the will of the people would only embolden those who opposed me. It was still too soon.

"Indeed. I was once in your position myself. However, stopping here would make you little different from Miyoshi Nagayoshi or Hosokawa Takakuni. Your reign would merely be temporary." Once again he'd mentioned names I'd never heard, but they were probably aides to the king in another world. "From your position, I gradually increased my influence, eventually transcending that of the shogun. You have a long way to go from here."

In this realm I had no mentor. No one, that is, but Oda Nobunaga.

"Hey, Oda Nobunaga. Since we're here talking, can I ask you some questions?"

"Sorry, but I'm not telling you the details about all I've done. It's more entertaining to watch."

This guy knew exactly when to stop. I wouldn't want to hear him brag all the time anyway.

"All right, then just tell me what it's like to have total power. That's all I want to know."

Someday, I'd have that power. It might feel surprisingly empty, but I'd be fine with that. I'd savor the emptiness of supremacy to my heart's content.

Oda Nobunaga suddenly looked a bit sad. "To tell the truth, I don't know, either."

"Huh? How does a conqueror not know what it feels like to conquer? Did someone brainwash you? Or did your son or someone oust you from power?"

"Right after I established my reign by eliminating Takeda, there was a rebellion, and I lost my life. I was going to be shogun, just like the shogun I'd previously installed. I already outranked him, so I had the right to form a new shogunate. To draw an analogy to your situation, Alsrod,

I was killed in a rebellion right before becoming king." Coming up with excuses seemed to have made Oda Nobunaga awfully chatty. "I don't know much about history after that. Once I awoke in the afterlife, I'd become a profession. In the meantime, the traitor Mitsuhide had died, too. Just deserts, I'd say."

I was a bit flabbergasted. "You call yourself a conqueror, but you really aren't, are you?"

"To the contrary! I'm a conqueror through and through! I was ninety-nine percent there!"

"I thought for sure you'd formed your own dynasty and ruled for decades, but you failed...and at the best part, too..."

He was actually getting pretty worked up. Apparently he wasn't fond of failure.

"W-well that's why...I want you to be king... I might as well see you through to the top, so I can feel better about my own situation. Mitsuhide's death alone doesn't do anything for me!"

"You're like a parent pushing their failed dreams on their child..." The new bond I felt was marred by disappointment.

"And what is so wrong with that? Your dream is to build a dynasty. Our goals are the same. So if you work at your goal, then the result will be no different for me."

"I guess that's true." I sighed. Even a conqueror was human, after all. He wasn't like some kind of god, but rather hopelessly mortal. "It's a relief to actually see your face for once, Oda Nobunaga."

"What do you mean? Were you afraid of seeing a goblin?"

"There's a reason you became my profession—we're alike, you and I. Some unambitious commoner could've never received you as their job." I was being guided by something, whether by fate or by the gods. I was now sure of that. "Kelara and Yanhaan must also have something in common with their professions, Akechi Mitsuhide and Rikyuu. That's why they received them. Everything is connected."

"I see. You really are as smart as I am."

Like I said, you're just complimenting yourself...

Of course, I didn't mind my profession telling me that. It was much better than no recognition at all.

"Now, listen well—go forth and make yourself king. You have what it takes."

Oh, I will. I don't need you to tell me.

◇

"—Excellency! Your Excellency!"

Realizing I was being called, I opened my eyes. Yanhaan was right in front of me.

"You were in quite a deep trance there. I never would have thought you would enter the tea ceremony's state of mind so quickly. I'm very impressed."

"Actually, I had a rather nice experience."

I had to be the first person in history to see their profession's face.

Just looking at Yanhaan, I could tell that she respected me. It wasn't quite like the reverence owed to me as regent—rather, it felt like respect for someone who knew the truth of things.

Throughout the ages, artists never truly bowed to someone just because they were a ruler, for a ruler who didn't understand beauty was no more than a servant in comparison to that beauty.

Thus, to be a true king, one had to know the real nature of beauty. The great kings of old had an eye for it and had considerable collections of art. Those collections weren't just displays of wealth.

Maybe this tea ceremony was an accidental rehearsal for something of that nature.

"By the way, Yanhaan, you didn't put any drugs in this tea, did you?"

"No, I would never. I may be an apothecary, but lacing the tea would profane the ceremony. If you want, I can drink the rest of yours."

"That's not necessary."

The fact that I had a unique profession was a miracle either way.

"A tea party is for spending time with other people, but tea ceremony is the ultimate confrontation with oneself. I think you had that figured out without realizing it. On rare occasions, people like you find themselves severed from this world."

I might have doubted those words if they were coming from a priest, but they sounded natural to me in the moment.

"Next time I need to make a big decision, let me do this tea ceremony again."

"Certainly. Mostly politicians have made use of it up till now." The dragonewt woman smiled cheerfully.

"I see. It seems you've met quite a lot of the capital's politicians..." I then proceeded to ask her what I needed to do to strengthen my hold on the capital.

"This is just me speaking as a merchant, buuut..."

Yanhaan gave a leisurely but interesting answer. She was no average person, after all. She'd have made an outstanding politician herself.

"Yanhaan Grantrix, I think I'll have a good position for you. Don't let me down."

Afterward, Laviala and the others did the tea ceremony themselves, but Laviala came out looking disappointed. "It was really bitter," she grumbled. "I just don't get it..."

"I thought elves had a special connection with plants, though."

"That doesn't mean we like things that are bitter..."

"By the way, was there anything strange about the experience?"

"All I can remember is the bitterness," Laviala said, sticking out her tongue in disgust.

◇

With the civil service exam's results, we had our first round of bureaucrats. Most of them ended up as low-rung government workers. And at the same time that they were dispatched, we prepared for the second round of testing. I had Kelara and Laviala helping me.

Kelara chose the questions. Laviala basically did anything else I needed, but she knew quite a bit about weapons and armor, so I borrowed from her knowledge to include questions about those topics.

"Surely you don't need to have so many tests? The government seems to be working with just the bureaucrats we have now. We still have some from before anyway."

"Laviala, I don't want more bureaucrats just so I can keep the old status quo."

"The more bureaucrats there are who were chosen by His Excellency, the greater his share of influence in the capital will be. I believe that may be what he's thinking." Kelara saw the truth with ease.

Laviala looked a bit annoyed, like she'd just been slighted. "I'm a soldier, after all. I never thought I'd come to the capital in my whole life."

"Relax. You know Kelara didn't mean anything by that." I soothed Laviala by stroking her head.

A new regent announcing policy changes just because he was new would definitely stir up discontent. There were always plenty of people who resisted change. That discontent would lead directly to government instability.

Looking back on history, many governments had quickly fallen when they provoked backlash for the radical measures they took. A government's legitimacy and usefulness were of secondary importance.

For example, reforms that raised taxes brought furious opposition from the people. Nobody would happily accept something like that. It would also be a bad idea to challenge the rights of the capital's nobles.

Human beings were conservative creatures. Change frightened, and the current king, Hasse, was a prime example of change.

Anyway, as for how I'd expand my power, I needed to increase the proportion and number of my supporters. I wouldn't make any changes in the existing power structure. I'd just steadily change out those in charge to be people under my thumb.

Hasse and his cohorts felt at ease because there hadn't been any changes to the system. They thought I'd be like all the previous regents—nobles who'd maintained their power while protecting the dynasty. By the time they knew what was happening, I'd have control of everything.

With the exams, I couldn't be criticized for picking favorites, since the examinees who were hired wouldn't be from my hometown or have any other connection to me. The former king surely wouldn't sit idly by anyway, so I'd quickly strengthen our forces. If the royal capital—not just Maust—was my base of operations, then total power would be close at hand.

Just then, Lumie and Seraphina came in.

"Ah, I see you really are coming up with exam questions."

"The princess said she wanted to observe, so I brought her here," Seraphina told me. Her smile was the smile of one who was plotting something.

"Well, well, whatever is the matter, my dears?" I said with joking melodrama.

Still, I really did have a lot of wives now, even considering my position. Aside from Fleur, who was resting in Maust after giving birth, my wives were all here with me. Kelara wasn't officially a concubine, but it was an open secret anyway.

"Yes, you must be a truly happy man to have such beautiful wives waiting on you," said Seraphina. "The princess is getting prettier all the time, too."

"Yes, I will make sure I won't embarrass you when I'm by your side, Your Excellency!" Lumie joined hands with Seraphina, smiling with delight. She seemed to have taken to Seraphina.

"And another one of your wives came from Maust today, too." Seraphina signaled behind her with her eyes. Fleur came in shyly.

"Oh! Fleur, I never expected you'd come, too!" I opened my eyes wide. I'd thought it'd be some time before I'd see her again.

"Yes, Lady Seraphina had it arranged..." Fleur was a brave girl, but since she'd gone around me to do this, she looked a bit unsure of herself. It's generally considered proper to keep one's husband informed, after all. "Forgive me for not telling you beforehand."

"Fleur, I'm not upset, so don't worry. Besides, this is one of Seraphina's schemes, right? You're not the one to blame here."

"It's not a bad thing, so I wouldn't call it a scheme. It was just a little…

project, is all." Seraphina smiled, really seeming to enjoy herself. The culprit had confessed willingly.

To be honest, it was a real comfort to have a wife who toyed with me like this. The higher you ascended in the ranks, the more distant people became. As regent, sometimes I felt like an executioner. Apparently to hold great power really was to be alone.

Fleur must've had a long trip, so I hugged her gently, stroking her bright-pink hair.

"How's the baby? Is she healthy?"

"Yes, she's with her nurse now. She's a little fussy, so her nurse seems to be having a bit of trouble, though."

"I see. This might be too soon, but I guess Meissel doesn't have children yet, so maybe our daughter can lead the Wouge clan someday. Of course I want to raise her as a member of my own clan, too."

"You're getting ahead of yourself," Fleur chided. "There is no way to know how things will go yet. We have to worry about what the former king is doing, too." On the other hand, she looked relieved. "To be honest, I wanted to come to the capital. I mean, you're changing history wherever you are, dear. I want to watch as it changes." She was a bit hesitant as she called me "dear."

"You would've made a fantastic general if you were a man... Too bad."

This girl had Wouge blood. They were an honorable line who had defended their territory on their own for generations.

"Then I could start training as a warrior now. There is no law saying only men can be warriors."

"I can't lose you in battle. No thanks. Even Laviala's almost died more than once."

"Oh, don't bring that up again! I survived because of my skills."

"Yes," I replied, "I guess there aren't any heroes who died in their first fight. There'd be nothing to record." All of us laughed at that.

Anyway, I'd figured out the reason for Seraphina's scheme. "You wanted to get all my wives together in one place like this, didn't you, Seraphina?"

"Ah, you've found me out. Yes, because you seem so focused on politics you don't have time to pay attention to your wives." She giggled. From behind her came maids bearing snacks. "Since we'd all be here, I thought, *Why not have a consort party?* The princess said she wanted to properly greet all your wives anyway. Though since Miss Laviala and Miss Kelara are officers, it's hard for them to get time, too."

Hearing her name, Kelara grimaced, as if to hide embarrassment. I hadn't technically made her one of my wives yet. She was more like a lover than a wife. Currently I officially treated her as a military officer of the Hilara clan. If I officially designated her a wife, it would be hard to appoint her as my officer.

Laviala was somewhat similar. However, her being my milk sister made her sort of like both my officer and my family, so everyone just overlooked that aspect.

Also, Seraphina had deliberately used the term *consort*, but that was something only a king had, so it was technically disrespectful. Nobody was going to tell on her for making a joke, though.

Lumie had a formal sort of look on her face. "Yes, I certainly would like to get to know everyone. Miss Fleur, I have heard from Miss Seraphina of your amazing insight."

She suddenly took Fleur's hand. When they stood next to each other, Lumie looked like she could be her little sister.

"Yes, I hope we can get along well, though I am ashamed of our difference in status. I am merely the daughter of a petty lord."

"We need not talk about that. We are all here to support His Excellency's clan." Lumie smiled innocently.

Next to them, Kelara and Laviala were dividing out the snacks. Seeing everyone lined up like this, I couldn't help but admire how capable all my wives were. Their desire to support my clan didn't seem like just lip service, either. It wasn't uncommon in history for wives to engage in diplomacy. They all gave me strength and love, although the latter went without saying.

"You look rather impressed. Do you approve of my idea?" Seraphina seemed pleased with herself.

"I do. I've been completely absorbed in my work, so it's nice to do a little something like this from time to time."

"Take the rest of the day off. Let's all chat over some snacks."

"My children are still little, but it'd be nice to bring them here sometime."

"True. Honestly, I'd like my child to succeed you, but we'll have to see. You'll probably have even more kids anyway." Seraphina's gaze felt almost like a warning.

"S-sure, yeah. We'll just have to see…"

Then, Seraphina stood on tiptoe and whispered quietly in my ear. "You haven't spent the night with the princess yet, have you?"

Don't say that here!

"Not yet. That can wait."

"Still, having too many lovers would complicate matters, you know?"

"That's not going to happen—uh, too much." Given the whole situation with Yadoriggy, I couldn't make any promises. If I mentioned I'd even taken a spy as a lover, Seraphina would be appalled.

Seraphina's party went on quietly and leisurely. My wives had fun talking among themselves, too. Fleur asked Kelara several questions about the capital. For her, it seemed, the capital was a remarkable place. After all, it was the setting of most stories for women.

"Once things calm down a bit, we could go enjoy the water in the ravine on the city outskirts," I said.

Laviala's ears twitched. "Lord Alsrod, I'm sure you realize that would be best avoided. Assassins can't all be stopped outside. What's more, it's difficult to close off all paths to a ravine anyway."

"I know. I wouldn't expose my wives to danger, at least."

"By the way, there is a major diplomatic concern in the near future." Laviala suddenly put on her officer's face.

"The meeting with Orsent Cathedral, right?" Orsent Cathedral ruled Fortwest Prefecture and was the greatest power in the capital area. "They can muster twenty thousand devotees from the capital area alone and up to a hundred thousand from all their strongholds in the kingdom, so I hear."

"Not to mention, unlike forced peasant conscripts, people fighting for their beliefs would be strong willed," Laviala continued. "They didn't used to have a lot of military training, but supposedly their troop and weapon qualities are getting better and better."

"Right now they're our ally, but, well, who knows what will happen?" I slowly sipped some wine. The sweets I'd eaten before made it taste bitter.

That lot ostensibly didn't fight battles unrelated to their faith. In fact, they actually hadn't interfered in the royal conflict around the capital. It'd be nice if they continued like that.

——Never trust the priests. They pretend like they're in the right, but the things they do from the shadows are pure madness. It's better to be open and fair about your lunacy, like me.

I'm not sure you can call that fair...but I know what you mean.

Religious forces were both a kind of nobility as well as rulers, and in that way, our world was probably not much different from any other. Assuming they were a group of pure faith would get you into a world of trouble.

Orsent Cathedral, in particular, originally came to power when a heresy called Orsentism, led by a man named Orsent, grew in strength. And the rank of archbishop had been inherited by successive generations of the founder's clan. Thus, they weren't really different now from the clan of any other lord.

New religious movements were fundamentally more likely to arise in cities, where there were lots of people. Urbanites sought out new religions more than people in farming communities. Drifters were more common in cities, too, and such people didn't believe the older faiths would save them. It was a natural turn of events that such a movement should arise in the populous capital area.

Once, when different royal houses were fighting each other, the king and his family mobilized the Neo-Summoners—a militaristic sect in the temples—allowing them to defeat the opposing nobles. Afterward, however, the Neo-Summoners set up a sort of vigilante group in the capital in a move to take control of the city.

Though it was only for a few months, the capital found itself in an extremely peculiar situation where its police authority was in the grips of the Neo-Summoners. The group held sham trials, apparently leading to merchants and others of heterodox faiths being killed. In the end, some capable nobles suppressed it, and most of the Neo-Summoners' leaders were purged. The situation had verged on disaster.

The Neo-Summoners had since mellowed out, but it paid to be vigilant when dealing with religious forces.

"Excuse me, Miss Laviala, let's not discuss politics right now." Seraphina chided us, thinking the conversation too difficult. "We're here to relax. You're going to give me a stiff neck. It'd be better manners to talk about these snacks or something."

"It's still my job... Cutting loose isn't very easy for us elves..."

"All right now, no excuses! If he doesn't take the time to relax, our dear regent won't have any respite from work; he'll collapse of exhaustion!" *Yeah, she does have a point*, I thought as I listened. "Here, have some more to drink, Miss Laviala," urged Seraphina. "Let's enjoy ourselves, like we're carousing in debauched revelry!"

"No, that would get us into trouble!" protested Laviala. "So many temples would be angry with us..."

Oh, for the love of... Let's not get too depraved here... It won't do my reputation as regent any favors anyway.

"Taking everything so seriously will only bring us trouble, though.

Not from enemy lords, but from elsewhere." Even Seraphina could turn serious at times.

"Such as?" I asked.

"There's a new king. Merchants are coming to the capital from Maust, too, and a conflict of interests is brewing within. The same sort of thing happened in my own prefecture, too." Three seconds later, Seraphina was smiling again as she went to get Lumie a drink. "Here, Princess, today's party is informal. Don't feel bad about getting a little tipsy."

"The nuns at the convent always told me not to drink alcohol…"

"Don't worry. Once you're past ten, it's fine. You'll start feeling good in no time."

"Hey, hey! Don't make her drink if she doesn't want to!" As I intervened, Lumie came and hugged me tightly.

"Alcohol still frightens me…"

"Don't worry, I won't let anyone force you to drink as long as I'm here. Seraphina, this is no way to teach a child. Do anything to corrupt her, and I'll relieve you as tutor and entrust her to Fleur!"

"You're right. I'll be more careful. But I would like you to be thankful."

"Huh? What do you mean?" At times like this, I couldn't tell if Seraphina was just being herself or if she was planning something.

"Look, you and the princess seem to be closer now."

As Lumie clung to me, she did have the face of a girl in love for the first time. "Your body is so muscular… My brother's was a bit squishier…"

I wasn't sure how I felt being compared with Hasse, but Lumie's long tenure in the convent meant she had never seen a man's body.

"I've spent a lot of time on the battlefield, so this is just the result. It's only natural that His Majesty wouldn't have a warrior's physique—after all, the king can't go to battle all the time."

"Th-that's true… But why do I feel like I'm out of breath when we're close, instead of relaxed…?"

I placed a hand on her head. "I don't think that's something you can learn in a convent." I decided I'd like to gradually get closer to this wife of mine.

I was a bit annoyed to see Seraphina smirking in the background, though…

That day, the palace was rife with tension; even the uninformed felt suffocated by it.

My first task as regent was simple: I only had to wait on standby next to the king. Up ahead stood the royal family's top vassals, whose families had served for generations. They could mostly be divided into two groups: those who harbored animosity toward me and those trying to curry favor. In the end, they were both pathetic, and I was entirely uninterested. In fact, I was glad they let me know how useless they were.

The remaining minority were both capable and effective. I could tell that much just from working with them briefly. The nature of my profession meant I could almost perfectly ascertain whether a person was exceptional or not. Besides, I had Kelara, who was a great judge of character. I'd never misjudge someone.

I would take in any of the useful vassals and gradually eliminate those who were not. Little by little, I'd increase the number of people I could trust. That would lay the groundwork for usurping the royal family's position.

"Sir Regent, do you think today's meeting will go well...?" Apparently Hasse wasn't capable of subtleties. He had spent his days living as a wanderer when he should've been learning how to be a king, so maybe he couldn't help it.

"No one in this realm is as illustrious as you, Your Majesty. There is no need to keep your pride in check, even in the face of a powerful religious leader." Hasse could only nod at my answer.

In came the leader of Orsent Cathedral, Archbishop Cammit—the man who most influenced the capital area's politics. He had to be past fifty, but he didn't look that old. At the very least, he didn't look like a genuine servant of the gods. Plenty of warriors made shows of piety in their twilight years, and that was more or less the case here.

"Orsent Cathedral desires a long-lasting friendship with Your Majesty. It is not much, but there is a gift I would like to present to you."

Among the gifts the archbishop brought forth were a hawk found only in the western lands and the carved shell of a turtle that could be found only in the western sea as well as milk-white porcelain.

"Ooh! These are some magnificent gifts! This is truly generous!" Hasse took them with childlike joy. I certainly wasn't going to upset him by telling him to calm down. Best not to put a damper on things. Denying him this pleasure wouldn't simply be a rebuke; it would make him lose face.

In return, Hasse recognized Orsent Cathedral's missionary rights as well as the right to collect a "god tax" in certain cities. Missionary rights had to be reauthorized when there was a new king, but this was only a formality. No temple waited for the king's permission to proselytize. The god tax was collected ostensibly for the restoration and repair of the temples. Naturally, repairs probably required vast sums of money, but any leftover funds weren't returned to the government. As a result, taxes were a big source of income for the church.

Later that night, I invited Archbishop Cammit to a banquet. Laviala and Kelara were in attendance at my side; the archbishop had two of his advisers with him. The tasks before me were terribly important, as he surely realized.

"I have long awaited the opportunity to meet you, young regent. No one as young as you has held this much power for a hundred years, as you know." On the surface, the archbishop looked like a friendly old man.

"That was never my intention. Assisting His Majesty in becoming king as well as aiding him during his reign, is simply the duty of a servant of the royal family."

"That is true. You have been busy managing state affairs, all while being very dutiful to His Majesty. This I cannot doubt."

"At any rate, it seems the cathedral has been successful in trading out west."

Most of those gifts of his had been obtained through trade. That is to say, on their way to the capital, those goods hadn't made it any farther than Orsent Cathedral's domain in Fortwest. Naturally, the archbishop had gifted them to the king as a display of Orsent Cathedral's influence. The capital area's wealth was even more concentrated in Fortwest than I'd expected.

Oda Nobunaga mentioned a similarity to some place called "Sakai." Did *Sakai* mean "border" in Oda Nobunaga's world? True, border regions did tend to become places of trade. The region west of the capital was also where the former king was hiding. There was a risk that Orsent Cathedral was connected with his forces.

"Those were offerings made by our devoted followers. We have many followers out west, you know." It was obvious we were both choosing our words carefully.

"Well, as an inexperienced young regent, I would be grateful for your continued assistance. I am still but twenty-three years old. I certainly cannot take care of this kingdom on my own."

I raised my cup, to which the archbishop raised his.

"I pray that you and His Majesty may have a long, peaceful reign."

The banquet ended with us both showing respect for each other—at least outwardly.

"There's something unsettling about that man," Laviala told me after the banquet was over. "He didn't speak a word of what he really thought. He didn't even try to threaten us, nor did he make a gesture of goodwill. It's rare for someone to have so little to actually say."

I agreed with her. She then sighed and added, "To think we'd accomplish hardly anything."

"What do you mean, Laviala?"

"Until now, your negotiations were always fruitful—in the end, you would learn the opponent's weaknesses or bring them to our side. This time we found little more than a sense for each other."

That was where my opinion differed. "We learned we won't get anything from them. I consider that a fruitful negotiation, honestly. It's far better than knowing nothing."

Suppose I'll make them reveal whether they're friend or foe.

◇

I ordered my officers Noen Rowd and Meissel Wouge to get their men trained to be able to move out soon. I also borrowed some of the king's most trustworthy personal troops. I could at least use them to defeat those who opposed the king.

The following month, I obtained taxing rights from Hasse for a number of cities in prefectures that neighbored the capital, and I dispatched a number of people under my thumb. I deliberately stationed some of them in cities on friendly terms with Orsent Cathedral. This essentially made it look like I was ruling the cities myself, so I expected there to be backlash, but things stayed relatively quiet for the time being.

Two months later, I sent troops to Sinju Prefecture, located west of Fortwest, for the stated purpose of attacking the lords harboring the king's enemies. This would be a proper fight—proper enough that I went along myself.

Entering Fortwest, we crossed the shallow but wide Sorret River. Advancing farther, we eventually came into Sinju. I ordered Noen Rowd, acting as vanguard, to refrain from capturing their castles right away.

"Excuse me, sir, but...why must we attack so slowly...? Your

Excellency will be rumored to be a weak commander…," Noen—who was known for being a fierce general—asked doubtfully.

"If we don't get them to underestimate us, they might always pretend to be friendly."

"Who would pretend to be friendly…?"

Noen didn't seem to follow my logic; maybe he didn't think there were others in the area who could be our enemy.

"It'll be obvious soon enough. If they mean to protect their claims on the cities, this is our chance."

Oddly enough, I didn't care what they did. If nothing happened, my sphere of influence would expand without a fight, and even if they attacked, it wouldn't be a mortal blow.

And then a messenger came to my camp on horseback. By his face, I could tell right away the situation was dire.

"Reporting! Orsent Cathedral has raised troops to attack Your Excellency!"

My generals were shaken. We had marched too far west. With Fortwest's Orsent Cathedral hostile, the way home would be shut off.

Not me, however…

"Yes, that's great news!" I clapped my hands and yelled with delight.

"How could you be happy about this?! We might be caught between two forces!" Laviala protested. To be fair, getting excited about news of rebellion probably didn't seem to make sense.

"Laviala, remember how you once said there was something unsettling about the archbishop? Long story short, you were wrong about him."

"Wh-what are you talking about? I can't understand you if you don't explain! And your other vassals must feel the same!"

Some of the others did look dumbfounded. Of course I'd explain. I wouldn't be able to put my generals to use if I left them in doubt.

"Verbally, the archbishop was hiding his intentions. In the end, though, he did the most rational thing. Thus, it's easy to figure out how he's going to act now. This may seem strange to you, but this is far easier to handle than someone more mysterious." I placed a rod on the battle map. "Tell me, why do you think Orsent Cathedral is so powerful? Surely not because they have strong faith?"

I looked at Laviala, though testing your wife probably isn't the best idea.

"Umm…is it not because they have lots of money?"

"More or less. Well then, as for why they have so much economic power…" I pointed one after another to the spots on the map with city names. "The cities' merchants and artisans, as well as the city leaders themselves, have great faith in them. Naturally, this earns the cathedral plenty of money. There are a few reasons why." I now pointed with the rod to where the names of lords were written. "There are almost no powerful lords in the capital outskirts. The land claims there have always been a tangled mess, so it's full of petty lords, you see. They could easily lose their territory if they're defeated politically."

"So in other words, it wouldn't do the cities any good to seek the protection of the lords?"

"Exactly." Laviala looked a bit pleased at that. She really needed to stop being so easy to read. "So that means Orsent Cathedral is the one with all the power in the capital's vicinity. Fortwest Prefecture is the only land title they hold, but the surrounding prefectures are under their influence, too. Many of the cities I received taxing rights to before are in their pocket."

"You mean you were trying to provoke them?!" Laviala's ears seemed pointier than ever.

"Well, more or less. If they wanted to betray me when I was at my weakest, I might as well make them show their hand. It's frustrating to have a big power acting so high and mighty next to the capital." If I couldn't at least put Orsent Cathedral under my thumb, I'd never really have control of the capital area. What good would a regent be if he didn't even have power there? "They didn't openly rebel right away, though. I guess it was hard to say anything when it's not actually their land. Or perhaps they didn't think it was a good time for war."

At the time, I couldn't yet predict what the archbishop was going to do. So I made myself vulnerable to attack. I deliberately deployed my troops in a place where Orsent Cathedral could catch me in a pincer attack.

Taking out the former king's allies in the capital outskirts would help secure my power, and if they sat back and waited, it'd be harder for Orsent Cathedral to resist. Besides, if they continued to do nothing to protect their cities, they'd lose the trust of the others, who along with their merchants and artisans might bow to me.

Orsent Cathedral had raised troops against me at the best time possible for them, so the archbishop must've had a decent head for military strategy. That wasn't everything, though.

——Damn, that's a hell of a gamble. It'll be great if you win, but if you lose to the priests, all the influence and power you've built up to now might collapse. Your power around the capital isn't secure yet, you know.

Oda Nobunaga seemed upset with me. *You're the one who told me not to trust the priests.*

——Even so, I didn't think you'd go this far to provoke them. You had the time to absorb the authority of the capital a bit more. You could have at least pretended to respect them.

I'm a warrior at heart, all right? To be honest, I ended up with so many troops that every victory came easily; it was boring. It's more interesting to win fights that seem even at first glance. Any fort would fall to an encirclement ten times their number. But the quality of the commanders doesn't matter then.

——I agree with you completely there. The battles I risked my life at were Okehazama and Kanegasaki and...well, others, too, but not many.

*　　*　　*

I'm not worried. After all, I'm Alsrod, not Oda Nobunaga.

——Pfah. I don't think you'll listen to me anyway at this point. Just don't get yourself killed. I don't want your campaign to end here, you know.

I mean, I don't, either. Being regent isn't exactly my final goal.

——Set a rear guard against the western lords and flee as fast as you can back to the capital. The priests wouldn't dare burn the royal capital.

"All right, Noen, take five thousand men into the enemy towns and convince them to cooperate. Kill them and raze the place if they don't."

——Hey! Why aren't you retreating?!

My official goal here is to clean up the area west of the capital. Once I defeat my enemies, I'll make a "victorious" return to the capital.

"Yes, sir! I shall be thorough!" Noen replied, brightening up.

His enthusiasm had been flagging recently without any opportunities to show off. Like him, many of my men desired battle more than authority.

"I'll attack from another road. We'll show them they'll die if they defy me, regardless of whether the cathedral is their ally. Feel free to destroy a few cities to teach them a lesson while you're at it. This fight will reveal who's friend and who's foe."

My commanders appeared heartened by my orders. Some of them were worried about what would happen if we lost, of course. But many of them looked full of excitement, like on the day before a festival.

At some point along the way, Laviala had grown pretty excited herself. She already looked like she was itching to let some arrows fly. We had come this far by vanquishing the enemies in front of us, one by one.

We were like a flower that could only bloom in battle. We ultimately wouldn't have gotten anywhere if we hadn't won our fights, no matter what schemes we hatched.

"I'll show you what I can do with the archers, Lord Alsrod! I wouldn't want to lose my skills by staying out of battle."

"Of course. Now go get me their general's head. But just"—I went over and hugged her, patting her lightly on the back—"make sure you come back alive. You're a mother, you know."

At that, Laviala's expression took on an unusual tenderness. She must've been thinking about her daughter, as a parent might. She always put on a brave face when she worked, but I knew she went to be with her daughter when she had the time.

"A child needs both parents," I said, "especially ours. She'll inevitably get drawn into a power struggle."

"Yes, sir. I'll make sure she and Seraphina's boy are both raised well."

"I want you to have more children, too."

"Lord Alsrod, you don't have to say such things here!" she protested, blushing. Laughter arose from the commanders behind.

Sorry, Laviala. Crude jokes are an old trick for raising spirits on the battlefield. You'll have to forgive me.

"Now that you mention it, I have a request for you as well, Lord Alsrod." It was just like my milk sister to come back with a retort like that. Her role as my sister had faded as I'd grown up and become more powerful, but that side of her still made an appearance every now and then. "Please set aside more time to be with your child. I know you're extremely busy, but please. Lately she'll ask me, 'Where's Papa?' from time to time."

"Ah... You're going to bring that up now..." I wasn't totally unaware, but I just couldn't help prioritizing work. "If we mess up here, you could all end up with nowhere to turn. I was just doing my duty as regent..."

"If a child is only raised by their mother, they won't listen to their father at all when they're older. Don't blame me when that happens."

There was more loud laughter; now I was the victim, too.

"All right, I'll think about it when this war is over."

"Please do. Don't break your promise, all right?"

"A regent never goes back on his word. They'll have to inherit my legacy someday, after all."

Once I beat the cathedral, things should be a little easier. We'd probably have peace for about three years, I guessed. We'd have trouble it didn't last that long, as I wanted to subjugate the east side of the realm before my kids were much older, regardless of what happened to the former king's forces. Who could say what would happen?

"All right, everyone coming with me, give me your best. We're moving out!"

Amid everyone's cheers, we put our backs to the cathedral and set out west.

◇

Of course I hadn't been neglecting to gather intelligence on Orsent Cathedral. I got frequent reports from the rappas as we were on the move. As I'd expected, those at the cathedral were criticizing my misrule and planning a pincer attack with the lords I was invading. Hasse was in the capital, but of course they couldn't really turn on him, as I was the one they wanted to overthrow.

If rebel forces occupied the capital for too long, the residents would definitely begin to complain, as was the historical inevitability. They'd have no choice but to subjugate the capital by force, oppressing the people's freedom. When that went too far, the people would get anxious to have the rebels put down. Making enemies of the locals would dramatically turn the tide of war against them. The archbishop—Cammit, or whatever his name was—definitely knew that much. So he was only thinking of defeating me.

Still, they likely didn't expect to get rid of me with this one war. If they could get good peace terms, then they won, and their allied cities would be happy. The archbishop probably wasn't hoping to rule over everything. He just wanted some power and nice benefits to go along with it.

I wasn't going to do things so peacefully. By assailing the rebellious cathedral's cities, I'd give them no choice but to fight.

In an all-out battle, I know I can win.

——You absolute fool. I'll say it again. You're even more foolish than me when I was young.

Oda Nobunaga continued to gripe on and on as we marched. And since he spoke inside my head, it was especially annoying.

You had your own trouble with religious groups, right? Unlike local lords, these people operate on vastly different logic. They're bizarrely unified and wealthy.

——You hardly have to explain that to me! The Ikkou-shuu were a much bigger thorn in my side than Takeda; they even killed my younger brother. They come at you with a united front. Lords don't have the power to make their subjects go to battle so willingly. They don't fear death, you see. They're insane. War is a struggle between those who fear death, but these people break that law.

The man really did understand the situation. My enemy was strong, and that was why I was going to strike first.

In our path stood a town not quite big enough to call a city, encircled by a water moat. It was in defense mode with its wooden bridges all raised, but the moat itself was narrow. It was practically a ditch.

"Right, who's going in first? They're hell-bent on resisting, so you needn't show any mercy."

"Leave this to me!" It was Dorbeau, captain of the Black Dogs, who gave the swift response. He was a werewolf man with countless scars on his face. He had originally been a hoodlum from Brantaar Prefecture, where he became the leader of a local mercenary band. Those mercenaries started serving me and became an official part of my army, then I added more men to their group and made them into the Black Dogs. All of this led them to be a relatively independent part of my guard troops. Of course, there shouldn't be much reason for them to leave me. "In return, I would like it if you let us loot whatever we can, though. We've had to be civil for so long."

He had more the face of a villain than that of a proper soldier. Maybe that was only natural, given his origins.

"Indeed. You've done well to hold back for so long. Feel free to go wild." I wanted to see for once what these guys were capable of.

"Thank you kindly. My men will be pleased."

"Don't you bastards go sullying the dignity of us guardsmen!" Leon Milcolaia, the elven captain of the White Eagles, furrowed his brow. Their personalities seemed hopelessly incompatible. Leon probably got along better with the Red Bears' Orcus Bright, even. Orcus was audacious, but at least his humanity was still intact.

"I serve only His Excellency, not you. Besides, battle often calls for a lack of dignity."

"You bastard! We were here before you lot ever joined!" Leon did aim for more graceful battles, but he could get pretty worked up himself.

"Let it go, Leon. I meant for each group of guardsmen to have different personalities. The White Eagles have situations they shine in, and ones they don't. That's all."

"Understood... I was out of line..." Leon relented.

"All right then, Black Dogs, give 'em hell."

Dorbeau promptly transformed into a wolf, as did his men. Some of them had fought alongside Dorbeau for a long time.

"Grrr...ruff!" Dorbeau let out a growl. The wolf sounds were his way of communicating with the others, but I couldn't make heads or tails of what he was saying.

The wolves poked around the water moat, jumped where the inner trench seemed shallowest, and clambered up. By the time the enemy tried to attack them with spears, the wolves were already inside. Some of them even cleared the moat with a single leap. I heard several screams right away. People with no hesitation to fight were powerful.

"Seems like a massacre. Everyone outside will wait in front of the bridges. Actually, that may not be necessary."

Once the Black Dogs were in, the moat instead blocked people's escape, dooming them to a pitiable fate. Flames were rising from the town before long.

"They really are a rough crowd, aren't they?" Laviala also had a hard time being happy about our comrades' domination.

"That means they're either done looting, or there's nothing worth taking. Then they'll burn it all to the ground. Everywhere they attack turns black, which is why I called them the Black Dogs."

"I wouldn't want to be on their bad side."

"It's important to have people like that as allies. Hurting your opponent is part of war."

Midbattle, armed residents who realized they were out of options crossed the trench and tried to jump out into the moat. The town must've been an absolute bloodbath. Of course, I had no intention of letting them escape.

"Fire!" Laviala ordered the archers. Flying almost completely straight, the arrows pierced foe after foe.

Raising the bridges and waiting for us had made their intention to resist unmistakable. If we'd bypassed them, they would've attacked us from behind.

"Laviala, show them no mercy. I always make an example out of the first battle. There's nothing to feel guilty about."

"Don't worry, I'm prepared for that. Besides, I've already killed many, so my conscience was never clear!" Laviala answered bravely, and she loosed more arrows.

With the inside and outside attacks, the battle came to an end in just about an hour. According to Dorbeau, the small town had had very little to loot, though. Taking people as loot was a thing, but since we didn't have the time to drag around prisoners, he said they'd killed everyone they found.

"I'm glad it ended so quickly. A long battle is more trouble than it's worth."

"Speed has always been my strong suit, just like you. Loot all you can and kill them, or kill them first and then loot—one of the two. Taking time to find the right approach will get you killed."

"If you were a mercenary, you sure must've been a sticky-fingered one."

There were virtually no survivors. My troops had surrounded the moat, so they'd had nowhere to escape. Apparently the town had been called Messe, but today that name had disappeared from the map.

I ordered the rappas to spread news of what had happened to the other enemy cities. They were gonna have to pull their hair out over whether to side with the cathedral or with me. Though neither the cities nor the lords would be able to abandon the cathedral so quickly. Still, once I burned another two or so places, others would start to surrender.

"All right, let's keep moving. We're just going to take everything by force and make them think there's no time to put up a defense. We're going to settle this, without even falling behind Noen's party!"

After giving out what rewards I had to, I wasted no time setting my troops marching. Most of the cities and castles ahead of us intended to resist. I'd take them down one by one, link up with Noen, and complete my subjugation of the region.

——I have no idea why you take such gambles. If you have trouble subjugating them, the cathedral's followers will come after you. Judging by the distance, if you're not mostly done in two days, it'll be too late.

If I have two days, I can make it work. They were all weaklings anyway, and I'd be attacked if I went back to the royal palace. I didn't want to ever be on the defensive, as that would only embolden enemy forces.

About five thousand jargs away from the first town I destroyed, I captured a petty lord's castle in one brute-force attack. I put Leon in front for that battle. After killing the lord's clan, I hurried onward.

The next city didn't take up arms and let me through.

Things were going well enough. I could do this.

◇

What awaited me next was a fortress held by the allied forces of two powerful local clans, the Salkais and the Friffaeds. It was Salkai Castle, home of Keenda Salkai. Their troops numbered about fifteen hundred. The fort was fairly large and constructed out of wood and stone.

I figured my fate would depend on whether I could capture it. Of course, I intended to do exactly that, and with ease. I'd show them the power of the Oda Nobunaga profession.

"It will be difficult to take this by force," Kelara, who was with me in this campaign, said without fearing my reaction. I much preferred that to someone who'd agree to attack only because I wanted to. "Behind it is a sheer cliff, so we can only attack from the front. Judging from the fort's size, it's sensible to think a fast capture would be tough under arrow fire."

"Kelara, if I were sensible, I wouldn't have attacked this far in the first place."

"I know. I am in your service, after all." Kelara put a hand to her chest and nodded. "So I think you will need to do something extraordinary. If that isn't possible, it's best to withdraw."

"There's no law that says a regent can't do something extraordinary, after all."

I slowly brought my horse back to my soldiers.

"Listen up, everyone. I'm going to take down this fort in one hour, starting now. I'm going to show them exactly who leads this realm!" I wasn't just trying to motivate my men. I was trying to inspire myself.

"I'm not serving myself here. This is a fight for the kingdom! These insolent fools will get the beating of their lives for allying with the former king and the cathedral!" Leading troops in war, you had to keep your composure, and at the same time whip your men into a fervor. Otherwise they'd never be strong soldiers.

"Let me hear who's ready to put their lives on the line!"

A tremendous cheer rose from them, like the wildest pack of wolves I'd ever heard.

Special ability Conqueror's Presence activated.
Takes effect when recognized as a conqueror by many at once. All abilities are tripled.
Additionally, all who lay eyes on you experience either awe or fear.

Special ability Conqueror's Guidance activated.
Allies' trust and focus will double. Additionally, their offensive and defensive abilities improve by thirty percent.

Now as long as I didn't fail to lead my men, I could win.

"Right, then. Let's come up with a plan. Generals, gather round."

I spoke briefly about strategy in a village mansion where we were temporarily encamped. "Laviala, you're an Archer, right?"

"Yes! If I'm with you I can't miss a single target!"

"How many in your regiment are Archers?"

"We have more since coming to the capital—at least thirty."

That would be plenty.

"Got it. Kill the enemy archers firing at us. It's hard to shoot up from below, but with your skill you can do it. Make every shot count."

"Understood." The smile disappeared from Laviala's face. It wasn't out of pessimism, though—I could tell a cold flame was burning in her heart.

"Meanwhile I'll dive in myself and break into the fort. Miss too many shots, and I'll be dead. My life is in your hands."

Laviala sighed. "I wish you'd be a bit safer, but that's how you are."

Next to her, Kelara was listening silently.

"Kelara, take a regiment around to the back of the fort. It may be on a cliff, but the enemy has to have an escape route. Some will try to flee when we attack from the front."

"I take it you want them all killed?"

"I do. Then the battle will end in our total victory."

Well, time to begin. Oda Nobunaga, let me show you how I seize power.

Leading my crack troops, I stood at the foot of the hill that led to the fort. The gates were at the top, past a long series of hairpin turns. All the turns were there to make it easy to shoot attackers with arrows. However, if they could shoot us, logically the reverse was also true.

I vividly remembered the time I went to Fort Nagraad on my brother's orders. At the time it was our fort that was about to fall, so I'd had no choice but to risk my life driving the enemy back by myself. I had so many allies now compared with then. The difficulty had lowered substantially.

"All right, let's go! Show them how terrifying your regent is!" I galloped my horse up the hill. "It is I, Alsrod Nayvil, regent of the Kingdom of Therwil! I've come to slay all who oppose me!"

I could faintly see the enemy's countenances falling at my words. Obviously they hadn't realized I'd come personally. *Believing you're safe is like being on a sinking ship—what military tactics book said that again?*

If the enemy believed being in a fort would allow them to hold out for a while, then I'd gladly shatter that illusion.

Their archers brought their bows to bear.

Do it, Laviala. Do it for me.

An archer who was about to fire was shot in the face by a long arrow. He fell backward slowly. The soldiers beside him went stiff.

"This is the power of His Excellency's archers! Who wants to be next?"

"Well done, Laviala!"

More arrows followed. Our attack left us fairly open, so some men were shot off their horses; far more of the enemy were getting hit, however.

"Get more archers!"

"This tower doesn't have enough archers!"

Panicked voices rang out from the fort. If they didn't have archers, we could easily make our way to the gates.

As they fumbled around, the first of our men reached the gates, and the magic users launched fireballs to burn the way open. Next to them, men set up stepladders to get inside.

At the moment, my profession's special abilities were dramatically strengthening my men. I figured if just fifteen of them got inside, our victory would be sealed.

As I defended myself and waited, the gates opened from the inside. I wasn't sure if it was because of my men or if my enemies were coming to kill me, but either way, it was definitely a great opportunity.

It was my troops who'd opened it.

"Your Excellency! Please come in!"

"We're ready for you!"

"Of course!" I said. "I'm not a politician but a warrior; see for yourselves! Everyone push forward! Destroy everything you can!"

An avalanche of soldiers spilled in after me.

——You did it. Lucky bastard. I guess you could say that's part of what makes a conqueror.

I wasn't exactly leaving this up to luck, Oda Nobunaga. I'm just trying to take the best approach. Besides, you didn't have professions like ours in your world.

With a good understanding of my own abilities and my allies' morale, I could make anything work.

The battle itself was over at this point. The castle really was going to fall within an hour. Now it was just a question of how much I could show off.

The soldiers with the three-jarg spears brought them down all at once upon the enemy. Their bones broke with a *crack*, and I saw them fall over. Their helmets had huge dents in them. A spear that long was also incredibly heavy. Whipping it at someone was enough to destroy their helmet. They were even long enough to strike an enemy while out of reach of their attacks.

"All right, I have to get in on this, too."

I drew my broadsword (and it was indeed very broad).

"Whooaa! Now, that there's an old sword!" yelled Orcus in his booming voice. Apparently he'd been fighting nearby. I'd selected the most personally accomplished soldiers for the Red Bears, which distinguished them from my other guard troops.

"This weapon was passed down from regent to regent. It's called the Stroke of Justice."

And indeed, the wielder's enemies would fall to prove his justice.

"Huh. I'm surprised it was still there after the regent has changed so many times."

As he spoke, Orcus swung his three-jarg spear, sending an enemy flying. They even flew three jargs through the air and landed next to their friends.

"Orcus, you're pretty sharp. You're right; I couldn't believe it myself at first. I thought it'd be long since lost if it had even existed. But I looked into it and figured out what happened." I gave the old sword a light swing. I was getting used to it faster than I'd expected.

"Most regents don't really go out on the front line, right? The peacetime regents especially may not have even had any battlefield experience. As a result, it was still left in storage from another regent in the capital."

"So you're saying that sword is seeing battle for the first time?"

"No, it has some tiny nicks in the blade. It must've seen some use back in ancient times. I guess it'll get to taste its first blood in a while!" I ran toward the central part of the fort. "Orcus! Come with me! It's time for their last rites!"

"Salkai and Friffaed are the lords of this place, right? Surely a regent of all people doesn't need to kill such petty lords?" Orcus ran without losing his breath. The fort interior was mostly flat ground, making it easy to run.

"That's one way to think about it. But if the regent himself kills the ruler of the fort, it'll definitely raise morale, right? I want to raise it as high as I can to take on the cathedral."

This was the preliminary skirmish leading to that.

"Yessir. Well then, I'll focus on helping ya!"

Holding my sword with both hands, I flung myself against a soldier trying to block the way, sending him flying. From behind, Orcus stabbed him in the neck with his spear.

"Yeah, it'd be nice if it had a bit longer reach, but it's not that bad."

First evading my foes' spear attacks, I closed the distance and then swung my sword. Once I did, they had no way to block it, so they collapsed on the spot. Even if they didn't die, I had probably used enough force to break some bones.

I swung my sword upward and yelled. "Listen well, enemies of His Majesty the king! I am the regent, Alsrod Nayvil! I'm going to slice off your heads and present them to the king! Come over here if you have the guts to fight!"

The defenders' jaws seemed to drop. They probably still couldn't believe there was a regent this brash.

"This is an old sword passed down by the regents. But they were all so spineless it never got used. As long as there are rebels preventing peace in the realm, I'll keep on swinging it!"

My men cheered. I didn't say that to rile up the enemy. It was to motivate my men.

A few of my foes did have some backbone—there was one unit that came my way, yelling, "Off with the regent's head!"

I glanced at Orcus, as a signal to charge forward together.

"If I die, I want it to be in battle, y'know. That's why I gotta come to places like this. Thank ye for all the good business!"

"After we get back alive, learn about tea ceremony from Yanhaan sometime."

"Oh, no, that sorta thing ain't for me…"

He genuinely looked disgusted.

"Aaaaahhhhhh! Orcus Bright, captain of the Red Bears—that's who I am!" Orcus went forward, forcefully swinging his three-jarg spear. A packed group of enemies who had been coming to attack were scattered. I then hit them with the Stroke of Justice.

At some point, the members of the Red Bears had congregated near me.

"Protect the regent!"

"Protect the captain!"

They went and pushed the enemy back.

I'd miscalculated. These guys' morale had been high to begin with. In fact, they were enjoying putting their lives on the line as much as I was.

Along the way, people shouted that a Friffaed clansman had been killed.

"Hey! Make sure you leave General Keenda Salkai alive! He's mine!" As I warned them, we were capturing more and more of the fort.

The tallish part with a short ladder was the highest part of the fort, apparently serving as the keep. The commanding general was probably there. The concentration of enemies more or less gave it away.

Our men swarmed it. The enemy's overall morale wasn't that good, so some of them seemed to be trying to flee out back, but the place holding the commanding general seemed to be the exception. They were fighting back well enough there—not that they had the skill, though. A steady stream of screams was going out.

As I was in the melee with the Red Bears, a middle-aged man with obviously high-quality armor appeared.

"You're Keenda Salkai, commander of Salkai Castle, yes?"

The man looked hopeless. The disbelief of having been invaded so quickly was written on his face.

"I see you are. It may be rather late for me to say this, but I still shall: If I could only fight sensible fights, I'd never have become regent at this age."

"I'll take you to hell with me, Your Excellency!"

Eyes wide, Keenda Salkai let out a sort of shriek as he came at me with his sword. I slammed my sword against it as hard as I could.

My enemy's blade flew into the air. As it did, I swung my weapon and took off Keenda Salkai's head.

"I've slain the traitor! This fort has now fallen!"

A roar of delight went out everywhere. Enemy forces would lose their will to fight now. I would be impressed if they could keep going.

Enemy soldiers were fleeing from the back, the opposite of the side we'd attacked from. Apparently there really was an escape route. Of course, Kelara's forces were there waiting for them.

My generals gathered to me. Laviala came back as well, with sweat trickling down her forehead.

"Well done, Lord Alsrod! Word of your might will get back to the capital, too! I'm sure everyone realizes how strong their regent is now!"

"You seem to think we're finished, but it's not over yet. I still have a job for the archers in particular." Just because the enemy had lost its will to fight didn't mean we weren't going to finish the battle. "Deploy your archers on the other side of the fort. Kill any who try to come back when they find Kelara blocking their escape. You'll be up high this time, so you should have a good shot."

"You are merciless, Lord Alsrod. I'll make ready immediately."

"I have to discourage them from opposing me, after all. I don't want to do any more assaults after this."

The soldiers who tried to flee were killed by arrows from Kelara and tumbled down the sloped escape route. The path was so narrow that not many could go back, and the ones who tried were killed by Laviala's archers.

"Right, we don't have much time to dally. We need to meet up with Noen's men."

I set my troops to marching once again. It'd be tough, but this was the outward journey. The journey home would be more exhausting.

I wanted to make sure everyone here could return home to the capital—but, well, who could say how that would go?

With no more lords resisting, we merged with Noen Rowd's five thousand men in the region's largest city. Upon requisitioning a building, I assembled my generals and listened to Noen's battle report straightaway.

"We engaged the enemy twice in a small village, winning both times. I have their head if you want to see."

"Later. Now comes the real fight. You took hostages from the lords acting compliant, right?"

"Yes, all of them. We've treated them respectfully as guests, of course."

No problem, then. The conversation quickly moved on to the subject of turning back toward Orsent Cathedral.

"Where might the enemy be lying in wait for us?" he asked.

"Their numbers are great, so they can't fight unless it's in an open area. It'll also make things hard for them if we make it back to the capital, since they surely can't go setting fire to it. That makes it easy enough to guess what they'll do."

We would probably clash with them on the plains near the wide Sorret River.

"Noen, how tired are your men?"

"They will be fine if they can get a little rest. We can keep going for quite a while. In fact, our victories have left them in high spirits if anything."

"Good. We'll be in trouble if we aren't at full strength for the real battle." I hadn't received any further updates from the rappas yet. "Now that we've joined up, we have thirteen thousand men. What about the cathedral?" I asked Kelara.

"They couldn't have been thoroughly prepared, so I believe they would have less than fifteen thousand at present," she replied. "However, they must be desperately assembling nearby followers, so if we wait too long they will definitely surpass twenty thousand—probably around twenty-five thousand."

"So about double ours."

One of my generals looked sullen upon hearing the word *double*. *Come on—if just double our numbers scares you, then you can't work for me.* I checked again, and sure enough, it was one of the generals who'd started serving me after I'd come to the capital.

"You look like you have something to say," I told him. "I'm not going to punish you or anything, so speak your piece."

"Taking on twice our number is most risky... Would it not be better to have His Majesty propose a truce...? Surely even the cathedral would have a hard time defying the king."

——Ooh. Now, this man's got his head on straight. Emperors and shoguns are worth using like that, you know. He's not exactly wrong. That's your best option here.

Oda Nobunaga's thinking was pretty sound.

"Your suggestion is worth considering."

"Thank you, my lord!"

"I don't intend to take that option, though. I'm going to keep fighting."

"Wha—? There are twice as many of them, and our men are fatigued as well... It may end in disaster... It is too risky a gamble to take..." Fighting the cathedral must've seemed awfully frightening to him, as he was trembling. The closer people were to the capital, the better they understood the cathedral's power.

"Just one correction: This is no gamble for me. I've always made sure

I can easily win before fighting. If I really gambled, I'd have lost a few times along the way, and I wouldn't be where I am now." I looked down at him, smiling. "Being a regent isn't so simple you can get by on guts alone. I'm going to send those priests back to where they came from. They won't be meddling with me anymore."

I'd heard plenty from Oda Nobunaga. Religious forces were stronger foes than lords were. I at least had to keep them from getting too full of themselves.

I planned to become more powerful than anyone else. That was what it meant to be king. Who'd want to be a regent or king forever at the mercy of the archbishop?

"I—I apologize for speaking out of turn."

Still, I didn't exactly feel like taking an enemy twice my size head-on. That would just make me a fool. I needed to pull out some tricks—and I had the people to do it.

"Don't worry, I'm not upset. In fact..." His suggestion to make amends using the king had given me an idea. "I should be thanking you. Don't ever be afraid to tell me your opinion. I'm on your side, after all."

◇

After the meeting was over, I summoned Kelara. I'd cleared the room of anyone else.

"What is this about? Is it something classified?"

"Well spotted. Put simply, it's something only you in your position can do."

"I think you speak too highly of me, but it pleases me to hear that nonetheless."

Pleased or not, Kelara didn't betray a smile. She was both warrior and stateswoman through and through. She never acted immature in any way. Even when we'd spent the night in each other's arms, I'd only seen the slightest difference.

"Don't misunderstand. I didn't just say that to flatter you. Even if I had someone else with your exact same skills, you'd still be the only one I could ask. Your life up to this moment has had a very important purpose."

"Forgive my stupidity—could you be a bit more specific?" Kelara bowed her head slightly.

"I'm sorry. I can be somewhat dramatic when I have a good idea. Now listen carefully."

As always, Kelara remained stoic as she listened.

"Do you really think I can carry out such an important mission?" she asked once I finished explaining. "I'm merely being self-aware, not self-deprecating, when I say my negotiation skills are lacking. I don't have a very interesting personality, you know. I received an education so I could correct it, but it didn't make much difference."

Hearing Kelara give her clumsy yet honest self-evaluation actually made her more fascinating to me.

"I understand why you're apprehensive. In that case, you can tell His Majesty this." I imagined the king I'd be usurping as I spoke. "'First, by demonstrating your military prowess, you will gain the people's confidence. There has not been a king for years who went to battle in armor, so everyone will think of you as even more illustrious than before.'" Of course, with Kelara's brains, she would have been able to say this anyway. Flattering the king didn't require anyone's permission. Thus, there was something else that was important. "'If all goes well, the regent will be in your debt. He will not be able to look you in the eye. Anyone who thought the regent ruled the capital will realize they were mistaken. This is the best way to enhance your worth.' Tell him that. If it's not enough, feel free to speak even worse of me."

Kelara's lips moved ever so slightly. My proposal seemed to have unsettled her, if only a bit.

"I would feel ashamed to denigrate you like that...although I do think His Majesty will accept if I say it myself..."

"Exactly. I don't actually want him to think I'm an uncaged tiger. I don't want his misgivings to make him join with other forces."

"Very well. I understand what you want me to do."

"Bowing to the king will be well worth it if it lets me take out my most dangerous threats." I was finished with telling her the plan. "Would you mind returning to the capital in disguise tomorrow morning? If it works, our victory will be complete."

"I shall do my best, but could you please think of a contingency plan? I would be overwhelmed to have your life entirely in my hands."

I went up to Kelara and hugged her gently with just my left arm. "Actually, I'll be the one supporting everyone's future. So trust me now. I absolutely will create an amazing kingdom."

I was the only one attempting, or even able, to do that.

At dawn, I took my entire force toward the plains formed by the Sorret River. It was about a day's march from the royal capital.

——Just be careful of muddy ground. The terrain was bad when I attacked Ishiyama Castle, too—it gave us a lot of trouble and caused some fatalities.

But you were attacking a castle, right? This is a field battle. I won't have to worry about how to assault them.

——Fool. That won't help when you only brought about half the men they did. You should have raised more troops for your little expedition.

If I brought twenty-five thousand men, the cathedral might not have made its move in the first place. I want to remove it as a threat. Besides, there's something I couldn't get if I did that.

——You want to create a legend, don't you?

Oda Nobunaga was really starting to understand me.

If I smash my enemy when everyone thought I had no chance against their numbers, people will think I'm some sort of god. They'll strongly feel they have to obey me. It's no good to only take a slow and steady "good government" approach. For better or worse, this is a world at war.

——I know how important deification is, but you should at least leave that until after you've mass-produced firearms... Ah well, I suppose it's too late for regrets. You have me as your profession, so you better win.

Amid his complaining, Oda Nobunaga seemed to relent.

I advanced my troops slowly. Along the way, I gradually recruited more men from the lords serving me. Even as they feared I might lose, they decided refusing me was too risky, and so they joined as requested. Being able to confirm their loyalty was nice, too.

On the cathedral's side, Archbishop Cammit was probably telling everyone I was going slowly because I had no hope of winning against him. It would make sense to see it that way.

I ultimately spent four days before setting up position on the bank of the Sorret River. The cathedral's forces were gathering on the bank opposite us. I'd gathered more men along the way, but even so they looked to have about ten thousand more.

Their forces were already divided internally. About half of them were under the direct command of the cathedral. The rest were under petty lords around the capital who didn't like me, as well as cities with armies. Apparently many of them were back to reclaim their land after being driven out by my arrival. Given refuge by the cathedral, they were probably anxiously awaiting their return.

Perhaps they'd also pressed the cathedral to fight against me. In the minds of the capital area's lords, the government was always getting changed in and out. The royal lines were just that transient, and regents fell even faster. Even when a new regent briefly appeared, he'd just get switched out for someone else before long. It made total sense for them to think that way given the history of this position. The current fight was also against the regent, not the king.

Said forces stood on the other bank of the not-so-deep Sorret River.

"So they're basically the anti-regent alliance," said Leon, eyeing the map of enemy positions.

A large map was at our feet, the river drawn in its center. It wasn't colored blue or green, as we hadn't had the time. All my generals were standing and talking while looking down at the map. I was doing the same.

"Hah, they're not that strong. Most of 'em are conscripts, right? We got plenty of professional soldiers." Orcus laughed, showing his snaggleteeth.

Leon promptly glared at him. "They may be conscripts, but all the cathedral's followers are skilled in the martial arts. If their soldiers were weak, they wouldn't be able to overpower the other lords. Besides, we don't have an overwhelming majority of true soldiers among our number, either. Arrogant bastards like you will be the first to die!"

"Good, I like 'em strong. Ya can't show what you're made of if you're not against the best, y'know. Besides, no matter how strong they are, these guys don't have the warrior's resolve. They're just following the strongest guy on the block."

I thought Leon was going to protest again, but he didn't interject.

"Maybe you could call it a warrior's willpower. Our regent is about the only one who has it. As long as he does, no matter how many or how brave they are, we'll win. I've always fought believing in that, m'self."

"I appreciate the compliment, Orcus, but I'm not fighting blind, you know. I'm acting logically, not on sheer willpower."

If one could win on bravery alone, I'd never have any trouble. Still, I didn't mind for a man as strong as Orcus to believe in me like that.

There was a big spot on the map labeled "Cathedral," but the enemy's positions were left unmarked. We hadn't been able to ascertain the exact placement of all their troops. The cathedral's troops accounted for over half of their numbers, so this was a bit of a problem—though we'd know soon enough anyway.

During the strategy meeting, Yadoriggy appeared suddenly. Her steps were silent, so she startled the generals who hadn't seen her arrival. This time she was already in werewolf—not wolf—form.

"The pack will move out shortly."

My face relaxed a bit at her report. "Understood. Then I can go full force, too."

"Also, on the way back here I found out who the cathedral's regiment commanders are."

Yadoriggy nimbly wrote down several names, one after another. Just as I thought, among the cathedral's troops were what appeared to be the names of lords.

They were a mixed force. They had incorporated the lords who'd fled from me.

"All right, everyone, we're going to make a final check of their positions now, but I only want you to focus on slaying the most powerful men of the cathedral. You can ignore the other lords. These are the strongest."

"Ain't it usually the opposite?" Orcus looked confused. "It usually makes sense to create mayhem in their ranks by attacking the weaklings. Deliberately going up against the strong ones just makes for a tough fight."

"A tough fight is fine. We just can't lose. We'll have reinforcements coming."

"Reinforcements? You mean Lady Altia's husband Brando Naaham? Or maybe Soltis Nistonia from Siala? Wait, they're way too far away."

"Definitely too far. Even troops from Maust wouldn't make it in time for this. Brando would have to go over mountains, too, so he's out of the picture."

"Then I don't think there's anyone left."

"No, there is. A trump card, if you will. Just hold out. Once reinforcements arrive, we'll be on top, so we'll attack all we can once that happens."

It would probably take the reinforcements time to march to us anyway, so if we had a hard time holding out, it could get ugly.

Guess I'll put all my hopes on Kelara here.

——You're a fool for entrusting something so critical to a woman with the profession Akechi Mitsuhide.

Oda Nobunaga was calling me a fool again. *Fool* must've been his favorite word.

Just then a messenger rushed in.

"Reporting! Enemy troops are preparing to attack! Their goal seems to be to assault our position from across the river!"

They probably didn't want to waste their food, so they'd made the first move. If I retreated home, it would be a victory for Archbishop Cammit. That would put him above me politically, and the cities' confidence in him would remain intact.

"Understood. Everyone, stand your ground. If you can just hold them off, that's good enough."

Now for the moment of truth.

Time to sow some seeds for a good harvest.

"I promise you this: If you can hold out to the end in this fight, we shall win."

Finally, the cathedral's best troops charged us. We fended them off with our long spears. They were slightly past the middle of the river, with the water just below their knees. With our spears massed together, they had a hard time breaking through. We just held them off until they withdrew.

Of course, as soon as they withdrew, the next regiment came to attack, but this too we held at bay. The enemy had more dead than we did, but it still didn't let up the attack.

Yes, good. The more fatigued your main force, the better.

The troops directly controlled by the cathedral were full of enthusiasm, making for a tough fight. We had a multilayered defense, so it didn't lead to a rout, but the places that were attacked had quite a lot of casualties—not to the point that any generals of note were killed, but at least one of the lords that had sided with me died. They really had followed me to the end. I'd have to promote their children later.

I observed the situation without moving from my position. This time I wouldn't rush out. If I were to carelessly dive into the battlefield only to run back, my whole army would rout, and I would be powerless to stop it.

"I see this is enough to put even you on the defensive, Lord Alsrod." Laviala seemed anxious as she assessed the situation, checking to see which units needed to be replenished with soldiers from the rear.

"Charging in can come later. If the archbishop thinks I'm trying to stand my ground, he'll take his time, too."

His goal wasn't to destroy me utterly, at least not in this battle. My retreat would be enough. Even he wouldn't want the regent to disappear, plunging the capital area into mayhem. If the chaos of war spread to the surrounding cities, taxes would dry up. He wouldn't be too pleased if a careless all-out charge led to the destruction of his forces due to some trickery of mine. Thus, he most definitely would try to drive me into a corner. He would invariably take the safe approach.

I wasn't afraid of people I could read. An ordinarily competent commander was no threat to me. What I truly feared was people with rock-solid convictions as well as genius commanders who acted on instinct alone. You had to change your tactics to fight those people. Fortunately, the commercially advanced region near the capital was full of people who acted logically. I could cope with that.

Evening came, and the enemy finally withdrew. The next day, they again attacked over the river. We stopped them at the water's edge. At the moment, we were fending them off, but if they pushed with all their forces, this would turn into an all-out battle. I was sure that wouldn't happen, but the ball was in their court.

The reinforcements I was expecting that day didn't come. I hadn't had any hope of them coming right away, but they were sure taking their time.

Had they been late leaving? It was possible they'd had trouble marshaling troops. Surely they hadn't lost their nerve? Perhaps they were too embarrassed about low numbers to come yet. Maybe that was more likely

I tried checking with Yadoriggy, but she just repeated that the reinforcements would definitely come. Well, if I doubted her, making plans would be impossible.

——Ahh, this is your fault for trusting Akechi Mitsuhide. It is Mitsuhide, after all...

Hey, you used Akechi Mitsuhide as one of your top vassals yourself. Have you ever considered not acting so arrogant all the time?

My expression calm, I kept telling my men to hold out for reinforcements. Some looked worried, but my guardsmen, with Orcus in front, had full confidence in my orders. We'd been in many battles together. These weren't the words of some petty lord who'd always followed the strongest person.

"Though it'd be nice if the reinforcements came on the third day. Some might start thinkin' about joining the other side," Orcus said.

"In a way, this could be a good chance to test the loyalty of the lords who were less eager to bow to me—although I'd rather not resort to that like some purge-obsessed tyrant."

© Kaito Shibano

On the third day, I personally took soldiers to go defend.

"Listen up, everyone. You only have to hold out! Don't worry about killing your foes!"

The enemy came even more forcefully than before. They must've thought they could end this. Or maybe they thought my side didn't have any will to fight.

I desperately suppressed any lingering doubts I had. No matter what happened, I couldn't show that I was worried. If my men's confidence in me wavered, my profession bonus would vanish. My soldiers needed to believe they were on the side of a conqueror.

But with the enemy attacking in such great numbers, my men must have some inkling of the situation, too. If they were attacking so boldly, maybe that did mean nothing was coming?

In the back of my mind, I had the idea to send an envoy to make peace with Archbishop Cammit. Truthfully, that would signal a clear defeat for me. With it, my influence would plummet. I wouldn't be able to control the cities. However, if I took too many casualties, the growing wound would endanger my ability to remain as regent in the capital.

Leading an army without showing any worry on your face was surprisingly difficult. I'd been going to battle so confidently for so long, after all.

…And then, just before noon, Yadoriggy appeared next to me dressed as just another soldier.

"The reinforcements have arrived."

"Arrived? …Where?" *Half joy, half disappointment* would be an apt description of my reaction in that moment. The reinforcements couldn't be here on the battlefield; there was no sign of any new forces' arrival.

"From the rear."

"The rear?"

"Forty-five hundred reinforcements led by His Majesty have arrived at the enemy's rear."

"Ha…ha-ha-ha-ha-ha!" I burst into laughter after a beat. "Right, right! So he took his troops all the way around to hit them in the back! That *would* take time."

"Yes. So as not to attract too much attention, I was told he also set the rendezvous point for the lords as another town, rather than the royal palace."

I was beset by doubt once more, however.

"So they're behind the enemy, huh? I'd like to confirm—His Majesty didn't say anything about attacking the regent, did he?"

It wasn't impossible that I'd been betrayed. Siding with the cathedral—which looked like it would win—was an option for him. Without the king's support, I would have no choice but to flee to where I'd come from. Whether that would end well was quite doubtful. Hasse had outwardly been gracious to me, but it there was no denying that I held some power. I hadn't quite tweaked the political system, but there would be little wonder if he wasn't happy with me.

Besides, Kelara was originally Hasse's vassal. If he'd told her this was the perfect opportunity to kill me...then just as Akechi Mitsuhide had betrayed Oda Nobunaga...

I looked Yadoriggy in the eye. Time seemed to stand still.

She opened her mouth slowly. "There is not a sliver of doubt that he is on Your Excellency's side. He is already assailing the cathedral, with the royal standard flying high."

I nodded, and my head flooded with a million thoughts.

"Well done, Yadoriggy. You're dismissed."

Yadoriggy promptly blended in with the other soldiers and disappeared from sight.

I raised aloft my ancient sword, the Stroke of Justice, and yelled, "You have endured bravely! Now it's time to counterattack! Let's crush the cathedral!" My voice reverberated nicely, as if my whole body were a musical instrument. "Listen well! All units will attack without delay. We're going to assault cathedral forces across the river! Ignore the trifling petty lords!"

With that, there was an instant shift in everyone's mood.

Laviala came to me with tears in her eyes. "It's here at last—the chance you were waiting for! I was so tired of waiting!"

I wondered why she was about to cry, but once I saw the others' faces, I knew. When I'd decided to attack, everyone had felt with their body and soul that we could win. And so they now believed victory was at hand.

They were right about that, and I was going to go prove it to them.

"This battle changes to our advantage starting now. Our headwind is now a tailwind! But do be careful as you attack. The enemy is still larger than you!"

My men's shouts were deafening.

"Lord Alsrod, I have one question!" Laviala approached me. "If the archbishop is there with them, what should we do?"

Priests were clergymen, so ostensibly they weren't soldiers. Generals who'd merely gone through the motions of becoming priests were considered military members, but an archbishop was unmistakably clergy. He was technically a noncombatant—and thus shouldn't be killed.

"Laviala, we may be fighting the cathedral, but a place that reeks of death is no place for Archbishop Cammit to be. He's officially recognized as an archbishop by the royal family, so he must be inside Orsent Cathedral praying for the victory of his troops."

To be honest, I hadn't been able to confirm whether he was here or not. His name wasn't on Yadoriggy's map of enemy positions, either, hence why I could say the following without issue:

"So," I began, "the archbishop simply isn't here. Should you see someone in a priest's robes, kill them without mercy." I could feel my men's morale rising. "Such a person is not a priest, but the enemy general's trickery! Anyone who claims to be the archbishop is fair game!"

"All right! I won't disappoint you!" Laviala answered emphatically, and she promptly ran off.

All right, time to get my hands dirty, too.

——Yes! What fun! This is what I live for!

Oda Nobunaga was whooping with joy.

——For a while I was worried how this was going to turn out, but if you can kill that damn priest, all my worries will be gone! Kill! Kill! Kill!

I hate to be the bearer of bad news, but there's about an eighty percent chance the archbishop isn't here. That was just a way to raise everyone's spirits.

I wonder what will happen if the archbishop really does die. At the very least, Orsent Cathedral won't forgive me until I'm dead—no, not even then. They'll probably be impossible to get under control. Not sure whether that'll be good or bad for me. If Orsent Cathedral doesn't stay unified, then I'll win, and if they come together and obsess over killing me, then I guess I'll lose. They'll probably invite outside forces to form a pact against me.

——I know why you were saying that. I just hate people who pretend to be saints. There wasn't a single real saint to be found back in my time. Several of them were much stronger than a cowardly general.

True. They're coming out to the battlefield, so they can all be treated the same.

Before I sent my men out, a horse came into my camp. Kelara was riding it.

"Forgive me for addressing you without dismounting. Kelara Hilara reporting—I completed my mission, so I have returned!"

"I wish you'd come a day earlier. You're to blame if this shaves a few years off my life." I was finally relaxed enough for wisecracks.

"His Majesty was too enthusiastic. Rather than a demonstration, he really did decide to lead troops to fight the cathedral, so the march was very cautious."

"I can see that. I never expected he'd suddenly appear behind the enemy. Do they seem worried?"

Kelara nodded. "When the different petty lords understood the situation, they shrank in fear, and it seems some of them withdrew their soldiers in an attempt to escape," she said.

"Having small territories makes people small-minded."

People with no redeeming qualities aside from adherence to tradition couldn't possibly point a bow at the king. Even if they wanted to fight a newcomer like me, they'd never from the beginning consider coming to blows with royal authority.

Thus, I'd decided the war would go my way if I got King Hasse to join me. Not even the cathedral had hoped to defy royal authority head-on. So now it must be in utter disarray. I didn't know who was commanding the cathedral's troops in this battle, but they definitely wouldn't give permission to kill the king.

"Half of the enemy have already lost their will to fight. We'll drive off the other half. Then we can go home victorious!"

I'd have to give Hasse my heartfelt thanks afterward. Usurping his power could come later. I had to improve myself as regent before I could consider that.

Once noon had passed, the atmosphere made a total about-face. Atmosphere controlled everything on the battlefield. If soldiers who were convinced of victory clashed with soldiers worried about defeat, the former would always win. Up until now, I had gone about most battles in ways that had given me an advantage from the start, so I hadn't been that aware of the change. It really was dramatic.

The enemy troops that had been standing against me—no, fearlessly attacking me—until the previous day suddenly had their backs to me, desperately fleeing through the river. They were sending up quite a spray. Arrows then pierced them, and they fell over. The river water turned slightly red.

The battlefield started to look like a mortal game of tag. Or perhaps that was the essence of battle in itself.

Special ability Conqueror's Presence activated.
Takes effect when recognized as a conqueror by many at once. All abilities are tripled from the usual.
Additionally, all who lay eyes on you experience either awe or fear.

*   *   *

This had to be thanks to my troops' belief in victory.

"Keep going! Don't relax now—we don't want the king to think his regent's men are cowards!" I spurred my men on while shouting at the top of my lungs. Soon we'd make it across the river. It was finally our turn to attack the enemy's position good and proper.

"That's right! The king is helping attack the cathedral!"

"We're in the right! We can't lose!"

"The cathedral is horrified, everyone! Crush them!"

Plenty of arrogant bastards had been hiding under the wings of the cathedral, so there were plenty of people cultivating hatred for it. It was now acceptable to crush the cathedral, thanks to this battle. Once people's minds had changed, we were in control.

Beyond the river, our foes were in greater disarray than I'd imagined. The king had probably thought I would just sit and watch. He hadn't provided direct military assistance to anyone for a long time.

I had Kelara waiting nearby, watching the king's troop movements. I had put her regiment under the command of another general this time, so she couldn't lead troops right away anyway.

"Kelara, you're the one who made the biggest difference in this battle. Well done convincing the king."

"His Majesty has always sought to change his lot in life—to become king and founder of a restored royal line."

"And you sensed his feelings and brought them to the forefront."

I was truly glad I'd put her in my service, despite her profession, Akechi Mitsuhide.

"I daresay all past kings wanted to leave a big mark and do great things. However, they didn't have the courage to act. For generations the kings didn't have enough battlefield experience to act spontaneously."

"So despite all that you managed to convince him."

"I wasn't sure I could do it myself, so I enlisted the help of your wife."

"Oh," I accidentally said aloud. I hadn't been thinking about my wives at all on the battlefield. Right—Lumie had probably never felt as terrified of war as she did now.

"Your wife entreated her brother the king to send his troops by any means necessary. I believe her zeal spurred His Majesty to action."

"I see. When I get back to the capital, I'll have to give Lumie the biggest hug. It's frustrating I can't do more for her."

"Perhaps spending the day together in her room would be the best repayment."

That would be difficult with all the work I had to do…

"I'll think about it."

Our troops penetrated deep into the cathedral's forces. For us to be able to get this far in, they must've had no more will to defend themselves.

It couldn't be a trap. Even if they meant to encircle us, it would be impossible with their men so flustered.

"Thanks to their earlier allies' retreat, their whole force must be falling into disarray. They're ready to break, I can tell," said Kelara.

"You're right," I agreed. "Given the circumstances, there must still be someone important around."

We advanced into the very heart of their force, but as they had no will to fight, there was almost no danger.

And then, I came upon a certain man—Archbishop Cammit, the ruler of Orsent Cathedral. So he really had come here.

Around us his men repeatedly cried, "This man is not a soldier! He's a priest!" Unable to run away before the others due to his position and abandoned by his useless allies, he found that his unlucky fate was nearly sealed.

"How do you do, Your Grace?" I said smugly from my horse.

Taking notice of me, the archbishop looked like he might faint on the spot, but somehow getting ahold of himself, he gulped and put on his most priestly face.

"Your Excellency, are you here for this foolish priest's head?"

© Kaito Shibano

"I've ordered my men to kill anyone claiming to be the archbishop, as the man himself couldn't possibly be on the battlefield. There's no reason anyone should complain if I kill you now, but"—I glared at him as he looked back defiantly—"I'll let you live this time. If you die here, your followers will forget about your blunder and instead turn their hatred on me. And people blinded by hate are exhausting. As the loser of this battle, you're going to apologize to His Majesty for your misdeeds. You don't have to die, and I don't have to be the subject of hatred; we both benefit."

The archbishop gnashed his teeth in rage—his was definitely not the face of a pious servant of the gods.

"Furthermore, I have one other reason not to kill you." This one might be an even bigger reason. "You never meant to kill me. At most, you just went into this battle hoping to teach me a lesson and cripple my authority. And so I'll let you live, too."

"I see. Thank you for your leniency."

"Next time you come to battle, come with the intent to kill me. And if I see you on the battlefield, I'll give you a taste of my sword."

The archbishop's men helped him onto his horse, and he withdrew.

"That was very generous of you."

I knew Kelara wasn't actually speaking her mind. I had enough political instinct for that.

"He himself knows it'd be better for Orsent Cathedral if he died rather than live in the disgrace of defeat. But he can't do that."

Cammit lacked the courage to oppose me unto death—perhaps because he wasn't a warrior, or maybe because there was no one to take his place yet.

I won this round, Archbishop Cammit.

"Now my—I mean, His Majesty's and my—authority has been established. The capital area, aside from the cathedral vicinity, will largely come to my side."

Finally, I can wield my might as regent for all to see.

After the enemy withdrew, I went and bowed my head before King Hasse.

"The rebels have fled with Your Majesty's arrival. This is all thanks to you."

I spoke from the heart. With this battle, my influence had risen dramatically. Of course, it would elevate the king's authority as well, but that wasn't a loss for me. The important thing now was that I get along well with the king.

"With pleasure. Now that you've married my sister, you're my brother-in-law. Of course I would come rescue you from danger. Especially when the archbishop was trying to humiliate a man who has done no wrong."

Hasse seemed in good spirits himself. This was the first time in forever a king had gone to battle, and it had ended in a glorious victory to boot. Of course he was satisfied.

"During this expedition, I defeated a number of rebellious lords. I would be most appreciative if you gave their titles to the people who helped make it happen."

"Indeed. I will consider it."

"Also, would it be possible for me to have control of some of the cities Orsent Cathedral held? The cathedral needs to be punished, after all."

"I see. I will think about confiscating them. In any case, why don't we talk more about it after we return to the capital?"

I bowed my head to Hasse once more.

My power struggle against the cathedral had ended in my victory, and the cities would naturally come to my side now.

——Well done…for getting out of this unscathed, at least.

Apparently Oda Nobunaga wasn't going to pay me a real compliment.

——If you'd just taken a little more time, you could have expanded your influence more carefully. But, well, your real goal is farther down the road, so I can see why you'd be impatient.

Of course I am; I won't stop until I'm king. Being regent isn't enough for me.

——Now you're in for a real fight against all the realm's miscreants, though. Soon the people who don't want you to seize power will ally against you.

I'll have to fight them sooner or later, so what do I care?

——Well, at least be prepared. For now…mass-produce firearms. Do that no matter what. It will help you in your quest for power.

You did mention that before. All right, I'll give it a shot.

Obviously the cathedral wouldn't be able to counterattack anytime soon, so things should quiet down. Maybe spending a bit of time on domestic affairs would be a good idea.

We made our triumphant return to the royal capital in high spirits. It felt like years had passed since I was last in the capital. Time seemed to pass more slowly in war.

The first thing I did upon getting back was visit my official wife's room. In fact, Seraphina immediately came to tell me to do just that. I wasn't sure what she'd say if I refused.

When I went into Lumic's room, my wives were already gathered there.

"Come in, dear. You must be exhausted after fighting for your life."

Seraphina was the organizer. Everyone was beautifully dressed. Apparently, they'd been sitting at a round table enjoying tea.

"Ahh, I had a bad feeling about this...but I just can't relax here..."

Laviala and Kelara—who as officers normally didn't dress up—were sitting there dressed like princesses. I wasn't the only one who couldn't relax—being made to play dress-up, they appeared to feel the same way. Kelara in particular was acting fidgety, as her dress was very low-cut.

"Lady Seraphina instructed me to come in this dress, so...," Kelara said, as if making excuses. "This doesn't mean I want to quit being an officer..."

"Of course not. I'm sorry you had to get mixed up in my wife's pranks..."

"Dearie me, that's not fair!" Seraphina was grinning impishly. "After all, Miss Kelara is one of your wives, too, so she has to help welcome you."

Kelara turned slightly red. I hadn't officially made her one of my wives; instead she served me as an officer, but that just caused Seraphina to tease her all the more. Somehow, I could tell it was just Seraphina's way of welcoming her, though.

"Miss Kelara, you should be a consort, too," urged Seraphina. "You're always welcome here."

"But then I wouldn't be able to go out to battle..."

And there was the rub. Sometimes the daughters of rural lords took up arms and fought when they had to, but for one of the regent's concubines to fight would only be considered odd.

Come to think of it, Laviala was in a similar position.

"I'm also not fond of this sort of thing... I don't hate it, but maybe if it were a bit more chic…," said Laviala, who was wearing a gaudy pink dress. If she were to show up on the battlefield dressed like this, the enemy might think she was some sort of god and cower in fear.

"It really suits you, Laviala."

"Lord Alsrod, you know that's not really a compliment, yes?" Laviala chided me.

Fleur, who'd been watching our exchange, giggled quietly. I would've liked to relieve my battle fatigue by lounging about with a well-mannered wife like Fleur, but with Seraphina nearby, that would prove impossible.

"Oh, so Miss Kelara counts as one of His Excellency's wives, too…?"

Apparently Lumie didn't understand much about this sort of thing. It was too soon for her to learn anyway.

"You don't need to worry too much about that." Seraphina was giggling again.

Standing was beginning to feel inappropriate to the mood, so I sat in an empty seat.

"Welcome home, dear," said Fleur in her pretty voice.

"I'm glad to have you home, too. I'd heard your situation was grim." Lumie's voice quivered with emotion.

Oh no, I really worried her.

Seeing her face, I felt a rare bit of regret. This wasn't just *my* life at stake; what would happen to them if I died?

"I really am happy I can be with you all again," I told them.

Renouncing work for the time being, I went on to enjoy a nice time with my wives over tea.

However, another grin rose on Seraphina's face. What was she up to this time?

"You must be exhausted from all this fighting, darling."

"In war, your life could end at any moment. You're on edge all the time."

I couldn't deny that part of me was addicted to it, but the feeling was likely something only warriors understood. If Orcus had been there, he probably would've agreed with me right away.

"That's no good. A taut string will snap if you never loosen it up. Maybe you should ask Miss Kelara or Miss Laviala about that?"

"W-well, in my case, I always spend my time on hobbies. Like watching plays if I'm in the capital," Kelara replied. Kelara was well-educated, so she had lots of hobbies. She was probably never bored.

"I run around in meadows outside the city to help me feel better," said Laviala. "I'd prefer a forest like where I grew up, but there aren't any near the capital. I just can't get used to life in the city..."

Their answers really showed off their personalities.

"Yes, and you've only just returned. You need to take your rest, darling," Seraphina insisted. "If we wives don't make you take a break, you'll simply keep trying to work."

I wanted to deny it, but I was at a loss for words. She wasn't quite wrong.

"There's not enough time in the day. I have much to do as regent, so no matter how much time I have, it's never enough."

"You're still human. You need to rest."

Seraphina did seem concerned about me. If I collapsed from overwork, she'd regret not stopping me, so she must've been beside herself with worry.

"All right. I just need a little more ti—"

Seraphina stood in front of me and produced a blindfold. "Put this on for a bit. Don't worry. I won't do anything bad."

"When you put it that way, I'm not quite as inclined to trust you."

"Your Excellency, you ought to trust Miss Seraphina. She is your wife!"

I couldn't argue with Lumie.

"Exactly. You ought to trust me. I'll cry if you don't, darling."

I decided to leave myself to her mercy. I knew whatever she had in store for me, it wouldn't be some hellish torture.

She put the blindfold on me, and I could feel myself being pulled somewhere. It didn't seem terribly far.

I felt a chill, maybe because Seraphina's hands were colder than mine. Even with her new social position, her hands had never changed.

I soon found myself lying on something soft. This had to be a bed. If not, maybe a chaise.

"Keep still for a bit, just like that. Don't go cheating by opening your eyes."

"I know you'll be angry if I do."

The bout of noise that followed told me they were up to something. I thought I heard voices talking, too. It couldn't just be Seraphina.

The bed was really quite comfy, so I felt like I might fall asleep.

"I'm taking off the blindfold, darling."

At her voice, I finally opened my eyes. I was on a comfortable canopied bed...and my wives were all lined up there with me! Notably, Seraphina and Laviala had slipped into nightgowns at some point. Fleur and Kelara had found themselves caught up in it as well, and Lumie in particular was blushing.

"Hey, hey! What is this?!"

"Come now, you see this sort of thing in paintings sometimes, right? Like the ones that showed how ancient kings lived, totally reveling in their vices?"

Sure, there were such tales in legends and myths. Some kings probably did cavort with their consorts, but...

"This isn't what I want... I've always acted in moderation."

If word spread I'd bedded several of my wives at once, my reputation would suffer.

"I know. Don't worry. This is just pretend—we're pretending we're the people in those paintings."

"I—I see..." I was a bit relieved.

"We were talking about how stressed you are, right? Thinking about how you need to relax sometimes, I came up with this idea. I mean, even when you're talking with us, you're thinking about politics."

"All right. I'll let you have your way with me, Seraphina."

For just a second, Seraphina seemed to look truly relieved. I'd worried her so much in this last war. News reached the capital only intermittently, so over the course of three days she'd kept hearing I was in trouble. My wives must have been terrified.

"That's it. Sit back and enjoy yourself."

Seraphina started calling me by the name of a mythological tyrant king, and then I had the bizarre experience of lying in bed with all my wives on either side of me. This may seem a bit cruel, but Lumie's obvious embarrassment was pretty funny. This was totally unlike her life in the convent, after all. The nuns would probably faint if they heard about this. They might think she'd been possessed and try to perform an exorcism.

"Lumie, you can leave if you're uncomfortable," I told her.

She was sitting cross-legged down by my feet.

"N-no... I'm your wife, too...so I'll do what I can—as your wife."

Looking in those brave eyes, I remembered something I needed to tell her.

"I heard how hard you worked to persuade His Majesty. Thank you so much."

Better to say this sort of thing as soon as possible, even with other people around.

"No, that was really all I was able to do..."

"I'm certain history has changed dramatically with your actions. Fifty years from now, people will be celebrating your efforts—that I can guarantee."

"Y-yes, sir..." Lumie smiled bashfully. My other wives seemed touched at the sight.

"Ooh, ooh, do you have any special words for me?" Seraphina nestled up to me.

"You should have a little more shame. And let me remind you not to put any ideas in Lumie's head..."

◇

Three days had passed since Hasse I had returned to the royal capital.

By the king's order, the activities of the five capital temples that belonged to Orsent Cathedral were banned. Soldiers carrying a copy of the edict went to the temples, evicted the followers and priests therein, and sealed the doors. The length of the ban was indefinite.

And this wasn't an idea I had put in the king's head; Hasse had approached me with the proposal himself. I was the one who'd actually fought the cathedral, after all, so he came to let me know about this idea.

It was a simple measure of retaliation, but not destroying the temples was clever. If he'd tried to thoroughly eradicate their sect, they might've tried to unite for another battle. If that had happened, the cathedral likely would've sought help from the former king's forces, no longer caring about appearances. At the moment, there would be no merit in diving into another fateful battle. We needed to show a little leniency.

I told him the ban would be enough.

Hasse said, "To be frank, I would like to tear down one or two of their temples, but as that would cause disorder in the capital, I decided against it."

"That is most gracious of you," I replied agreeably.

Radical actions always begat a strong backlash. My power wasn't secure enough yet for me to subdue it without any trouble. Eventually I'd probably clash with the cathedral, but when that happened I just had to win.

Ten days after my triumphant return, an envoy came from Orsent Cathedral to apologize for defying the king as well as to petition for the emancipation of the cathedral's temples. I was in attendance.

I left the questioning to Kelara and Yanhaan. I'd added Yanhaan because I thought it might help ease tensions. As an expert in tea ceremony, this dragonewt woman was always very laid-back. It was quite hard to believe she was a successful merchant. Actually, maybe putting the other party at ease was the key to business negotiations.

"Soooo why did the cathedral engage in this, you knooow, struggle?"

I'd instructed Yanhaan to speak even more slowly than usual.

"W-well…many of the lords the regent attacked were followers of our teachings, so it was to aid them…"

Of course they couldn't admit it had been to protect their interests in the cities and taxes. This sounded more acceptable.

"I see. However, aaaall the lords His Excellency attacked had ignored their writs of revocation and calls for surrender, which appears fairly unreasonable, soooo what do you have to say about that? Surely it is not righteous to aid your followers against reason?"

Yanhaan came across as very casual, but she knew exactly what to point out.

"No...it is nothing like that..."

"Servants of the gods would never support people without principles, would theeey? Judging from thaaat, you came to apologize because you lost, but you have noooo remorse for your actions, and you think you are in the right. Is that what I am to understaaand?"

Yanhaan's oddly languid speech didn't sound accusatory at all. The message, however, was thoroughly so.

This was how merchants did things. They brought the other person in line with their own rhythm, and moved the conversation forward from there. It must've been harder for the envoy to deal with than a by-the-book bureaucrat.

"Not at all, not at all... What happened was...the lords were in the wrong, but we thought the punishment to be too harsh, so we wanted to alleviate it..." The envoy was faltering under the criticism.

I think I'll have plenty of use for you, Yanhaan.

"Indeeeed. I understand your point."

The envoy looked relieved.

"However...looking into it, it certainly appears as if the cathedral raised troops for the sake of its incooome. Is money more important than your faaaith?" Yanhaan pulled out some sort of document.

"That is impossible..."

"Like when I see the prayers Archbishop Cammit performed in a certain city and the donations given for it, it just looks as if you have a vested iiinterest."

"No, I'm sure that city just made a large donation out of piety…"

The envoy dripped cold sweat as he continued to try to explain himself. Having gathered more documents than I'd imagined, Yanhaan went on to ask forthrightly about the things she found unusual. And yet, she often yawned as she listened to him speak.

The envoy had to say that they'd been wrong to fight while explaining that their beliefs weren't wrong. It was contradictory, but that was all he could say. He certainly couldn't admit they didn't care about their beliefs.

This piqued Yanhaan's interest, and the conversation somehow turned into something like a theological debate. Apparently Yanhaan was quite well versed in scripture, as she gave several specific people's names.

"…Thus, aren't the things Orsent Cathedral saying hereticaaal? Compared with your ooown teachings, at least."

"Not at all… For example…I forget exactly which scripture it is, but…"

——Ahh, this reminds me of all the trouble I gave the priests of a certain sect. I wonder if this counts as persecution, too.

You did something like this, too, Oda Nobunaga?

——I set up a special place for it. I've never heard of forcing such a discussion on someone who came to apologize.

I guess it's just Yanhaan's personality.

——Just seeing priests in the pit of despair brings me satisfaction, so I don't mind it. Those damn priests are liars. On the other hand, that woman with dragon horns is honest. I don't know if gods really exist, but if they do, they'd favor the honest.

Yeah, that's true. We're the ones in the right.

We went ahead and accepted the envoy's explanation, and Orsent Cathedral agreed to give up quite a few of its cities and pay reparations to the king.

Finally, I could extend my power to the area around the capital.

◇

After we were done tormenting the cathedral's envoy, I went to Yanhaan's manor for another tea ceremony. I entered the minuscule little room and drank the green-colored tea that Yanhaan passed me from across the table.

That's all it was, but completely unlike during a tea party, there was a mysterious tension hanging in the air. Perhaps Yanhaan had taken hints from some secret religious rituals.

Last time, I'd found myself face-to-face with Oda Nobunaga, though I wasn't quite sure why that sort of thing had happened.

"How is it?"

During tea ceremony, Yanhaan seemed somehow more mature—not with an alluring charm, but the opposite, with something like the purity of a saint.

"It tastes better than it did last time. Like it cleanses me by washing the gunk left in my mouth into my stomach."

"That's good. I'm happy to hear that, especially as the host."

Having taken a breather, I could finally get to the main topic.

"I realized something as I watched you work today. You're too good to just be a hobbyist and merchant. I want you to formally assist me in my ambitions." This foreign woman would definitely prove useful.

"Yes, that's why I took the exam."

Yanhaan drank the tea she'd poured herself. It occurred to me that the action suited her awfully well, maybe thanks to her Sen no Rikyuu profession.

I'd had a very clear realization after getting to the royal capital. People with unique professions usually had useful and unconventional strengths. The dwarf Ortonba with his Kunitomo Shuu profession. Kelara with her Akechi Mitsuhide profession. I wanted more people like that among my vassals.

"I want to see the world in aaall its charm. That's why I came to this realm—in a word, because it was wild."

"You're an odd one." I smiled, but I doubt it reached my eyes—I'd felt exactly the same way. I must've been bored with this world. It was ridiculous to have lived in fear because I was born to a petty lord's clan that could be wiped out at any time. Maybe I'd had more aspirations than the average peasant, but my life definitely hadn't been interesting or fun.

In that case, I might as well try to be king, even if it was dangerous. That was how I lived my life. Yanhaan the apothecary might not try to be king, but our thoughts were probably similar.

"I came here because I thought you would be the person who would make this world interesting for me. The path you seek is unlike that of anyone else."

Alone with me in this room, Yanhaan didn't call me "Your Excellency." Formal hierarchy had no place here.

"You really do understand. I intend to at least end this eternal game of puppets and rulers constantly switching in and out of power. I don't exactly have a plan for after that, but still, my coronation alone will change this kingdom. Er, I suppose 'this kingdom' will be gone then."

"Yes, and tea ceremony is especially suited for such a new world. This is no antiquated waste of time."

Yanhaan had said she came to this realm from another land. In other words, with her background, she fundamentally had no interest in our past. Such people were more trustworthy when it came to carrying out big plans. People stuck in the past would definitely be afraid, as I'd be erasing it.

"Do you know much about politics, Yanhaan?"

"I'm not sure if I know how to answer thaaat, but as an outsider, I suppose I can see things from an outside point of view."

All right, you pass.

"I think I'll be putting you to great use. I knew that exam would be worthwhile; it's how I found you."

"Yes, and if you wish to reward me, nothing would please me more than receiving your help in spreading my tea philosophy. These days I'm more interested in this than my job as a merchant."

"That's a hell of a bargain."

Afterward, we discussed whom I should dispatch to my newly subordinate cities and territory. Yanhaan suggested the names of several bureaucrats. Many of them had passed the exam just the other day. I asked her how she knew so much.

"Doing business and holding tea ceremonies in the capital makes for looots of connections. I have plenty more where that came from."

I wanted Yanhaan more than ever.

"Say, you don't have a husband, do you?"

"I'm afraid nooot. I just wanted to enjoy my work as a merchant, so I've still never fallen for anyone or been fallen for."

"Will you be my wife?"

I figured that if Yanhaan was part of my consort, she would run things there smoothly for me. Seraphina was clever, but she could be a bit pushy at times. It was worrisome.

"As much as that pleases me to hear, if I did become your wife, then I wouldn't be able to work as a merchant anymore, you knooow." She gently refused me. She must've taken it as a joke. "As a lover, however...I suppose that would depend on the mood," she added aloofly, without changing her facial expression.

"Crafty girl."

"Tea is the best of crafts, you knooow. Also, please promise me one thing. The ceremony site is sacred, so no getting intimate while we're here."

"Sure. I wouldn't want to disrespect your values."

After we left the small tea-ceremony room, Yanhaan led me to her bedroom. Dragonewts had remarkably supple skin.

Even in bed, I asked her a few questions on politics. Compared with my more concrete and pressing questions during the tea ceremony, the problems we discussed here were more long-term.

"I think you should take things slowly for a few yeeears. That's how long it takes for one's power to stabilize."

"You're right. I'll keep that in mind."

I don't need to make any big attacks soon, so maybe I'll see how things go for about three years.

Of course, I wasn't going to do nothing. I was going to sow the seeds I needed.

Harvest time couldn't come fast enough.

It was past midsummer now.

I returned to my hometown and clan birthplace, Nayvil County in Fordoneria Prefecture. I was shocked to see Nayvil Castle looking far more miserable than I'd imagined.

"Hey, Laviala, was our old headquarters always this tiny?"

"It feels shabby to me, too. Back then, I thought it was much bigger..."

"I thought I'd feel at least some nostalgia when I got here, but I don't at all."

"Of course you don't. After all, you weren't the lord of this castle for very long. Wouldn't you have more memories in the manor you used to live in?" I realized she was right. "Do you want to visit the manor while we're here?"

"No, it's fine. I'm here to visit my clan's graves."

"How admirable to cherish your hometown so." Kelara's compliment was genuine, not an attempt at brownnosing. She even seemed happy.

"Yes, I wanted to do something that would truly please someone like you. I've moved on a bit too far from here, after all."

People who left were looked down on. The nail that sticks out gets hammered down, as they say. I must've had lots of enemies by now.

"So I came to at least show I'm not neglecting my hometown."

"I know. Besides, you seem to be enjoying yourself." Kelara appeared to have read my mind.

Strangely, I found myself shedding a few tears as I gazed at the castle where I'd been the lord of a few mere counties.

"I sure did well to come from a place like this all the way to managing kingdom affairs. Actually, I guess I started from an even worse position."

Hardly anyone from Nayvil was in my military now. Most had come in after I'd expanded my territory. In other words, I didn't have any vassals from my time in Nayvil. Not that there were many people with this place as their hometown, though...

I heard someone crying, for some reason.

"Kelara, why are you crying, too?" Kelara, who was always calm and collected, had tears streaming down her cheeks like a court lady.

"A good question... Perhaps I found myself sympathizing with you? It must have been a long and hard fight."

A few others were crying, too. It was rather awkward seeing people besides myself getting emotional.

I turned toward my vassals and said, "Everyone, thank you from the bottom of my heart for serving me all this time. I sure never thought I'd rise to my current position from a place like this. I even felt like I was going to die a meaningless death in that tiny fort that was about to fall."

The sun felt just right as it shone on me. Maybe the weather had something to do with it, but this was the calmest I'd felt in years.

"After I survived, I fought desperately to get stronger. I did everything I could, even getting my hands dirty. But it seems my efforts have finally been rewarded. This is all thanks to you, all of you who supported me. I couldn't have come this far by myself." It must've been unprecedented for a regent, but I bowed my head slowly. "Thank you. And please keep up the good work."

From seemingly no one in particular, I heard the words, "The pleasure is ours!" followed by similar shouts one after another.

I knew I was a selfish man, but I did want to fight alongside my vassals as long as I could.

*　　*　　*

The next day, we went to the Nayvil clan's ancestral cemetery. The graves were well tended, but none of them were very big. My ancestors' social standing prevented them from being able to erect more luxurious graves. They were the low, rounded tombstones you saw everywhere. I'd passed by many a grave during my expedition, and so many of them had this type of petty lord's grave marker.

This was just a visit, so not only were my vassals with me, but so were my wives. Lumie was my legal wife, so I had her right next to me. On my other side waited Seraphina and Fleur.

"I have reached the rank of regent, my clansmen. Which one am I again—the sixteenth? I shall do everything I can to make my line prosper, starting with me."

The people around me were offering a prayer along with me. A hushed silence went on for some time.

"You know, these graves could be renovated into something far more impressive. What do you think?" Lumie asked. For someone from the royal family, this graveyard must have been a real shock. "Won't you at least make the tombstones bigger for more words? Then people can celebrate the Nayvils for many years."

"No, they're fine as they are, Lumie. I hear it's unlucky to make graves too fancy anyway." I shook my head and refused her suggestion. "Besides, I have certain plans for the future. There's word of a famine happening out west, too, so it'd be unsavory to do anything too extravagant."

The period before harvest was the time when foodstuffs were most scarce. Famines had been especially frequent recently.

"But that's outside of Your Excellency's territory. I'm talking about inside your territory, where the former king's friends are."

"As regent, I have to think about the realm in its entirety. That's what a regent does."

Lumie let out an "Ah…"

"You really do understand your duties, darling." Seraphina came closer to me. "That's right. You're not done yet. You have to shoot for even higher up. Please become king soon."

"Well, that's what I meant, but you don't really need to say that out loud..." I'd do something with my ancestors' graves after I became king.

After visiting the graves, we took a tour of the domain by carriage, and as we did, people welcomed me from the roadside.

"Seraphina, you had something to do with this, didn't you?"

"It wasn't me. This is the work of Fleur."

Fleur nodded softly. "I couldn't make it to the royal capital for a while, so I wanted to get a look at some of Maust and Nayvil."

"That's so thoughtful of you. Thanks so much."

Childbirth had kept Fleur from coming to the capital right away, but it seemed she'd made good use of the time.

"Also, I didn't quite plan it. As Your Excellency's hometown, Nayvil County has had lower taxes, too, so of course everyone loves you."

I laughed at my wasted gratitude.

"I guess so. There's no better lord than one who lowers taxes."

"Of course, you were also quite popular to begin with. There's no way someone so young and skilled at war wouldn't have the confidence of his people."

"You're to thank for keeping a good eye on things while I was away."

While I'd been away from Maust Castle, I'd left some of the governance to Fleur. Of course, because I was lord, most official documents had been issued under my name, but I'd left some of the actual decision-making to Fleur. That's how intelligent she was. If she hadn't been my wife, I'd have liked to use her as a civil servant.

"I did everything in my power to fulfill what you asked of me, but I think many people were unhappy with it. There must be plenty of people who think a woman shouldn't be governing."

Fleur wasn't smiling as she spoke. She was speaking purely from a bureaucratic point of view, not complaining about a lack of popularity.

"People like that would find another reason to complain even if I did things myself. Don't worry about it. It's normal for a clan head's wife to do things on his behalf when he's away anyway."

"Yes, that's true. It goes back at least eight hundred years to the wife of a margrave. When I glanced through the records, I found at least ten more cases after that."

So she'd even checked for precedents. Not to sound full of myself, but she'd made the right choice being my wife. Living under a small viscount-level clan, she wouldn't have had the opportunity to show what she was capable of.

"Thanks. I can't wait to get back to Maust Castle."

After my inspection of the Nayvil clan's birthplace, I had plans to go to my domain capital, Maust Castle. Lords from all over were going to come to celebrate me. Since I'd been spending all my time in the royal capital, this would also help me rein things in. Many of the people who had become regent only to fall did so because they neglected their hometown.

It was understandable. The regent was basically at the top of the vassal ladder. His actual power often surpassed that of the king.

Getting so used to life in the royal capital made a person forget about their home base—and when that happened, someone was bound to show up there with machinations of their own. It was that kind of era. You couldn't let your guard down.

"I don't think there have been any changes with regard to Maust Castle, but…" Fleur seemed to be choosing her words a bit carefully. "I believe many of the surrounding lords are afraid of you, Your Excellency. For a long time, none of them have experienced having to obey someone so powerful."

"Understood. I'll try to be careful."

Needless to say, my reception in Maust Castle town far outstripped that of Nayvil County. My entrance into the castle had to be ceremonial;

I couldn't just walk in without any fanfare. I had come back from the royal capital, after all, so it was a triumphant return if there ever was one.

"It's getting there, but it's not quite like the royal capital yet," I muttered as I rode my horse through the castle town. "Someday, I'll make this city even grander than the capital—and make it the new capital, or at least like a secondary one."

"Some governments have collapsed after their capital relocation caused them to lose the people's trust. I wouldn't quite recommend it," Kelara admonished.

"I was just saying it. Besides, that's all up to His Majesty to decide."

"Indeed. If he ever suggests we move the capital to Maust, let's give it another thought." Kelara now fell silent with the mention of the king.

Back in Maust Castle for the first time in forever, I waited for the appointed day.

Lords came one after another, mainly from the surrounding area, to celebrate my victory against Orsent Cathedral. Including those with smaller territories, there were about forty of them—more than I'd thought.

Some of them—like my sister Altia's husband, Brando Naaham, and Seraphina's father, Ayles Caltis—were practically my fellow clansmen. I believed I'd given them ranks befitting that relationship. Fleur's brother, Meissel Wouge, was also more or less family, though he was technically just my general.

Going before the lords, who were lined up, I sat down and said magnanimously, "There is no greater honor as regent than to have my victory celebrated by all of you."

However, I spotted one among them who didn't look very thrilled. It was Brando, Altia's husband. What was he looking so sour for?

"My brother-in-law, I think this glorious victory is truly magnificent," Brando said to me. "However...I must ask...isn't it a bit odd how high your chair is?"

"My chair? Ahh, I changed it to fit my new status as regent. If I don't conduct myself as a regent, people might think I'm disrespecting royal authority."

Brando didn't seem satisfied with that. "Right. But this…doesn't it make us look like we're your vassals, rather than your allies…?"

Ahh, so that's what this is about.

I knew what Brando meant now. In other words, he thought the lords were purely my allies, rather than this being a liege-and-vassal relationship. To be fair, no matter how big the difference in our amount of land or soldiers, it didn't mean Brando and I had a liege-and-vassal relationship. All of us were independent lords.

So then whom did they serve? Of course, it was the king. Everyone was beneath Hasse I now. Thus, Brando's discontent was not baseless. Even if I was regent, they didn't have to consider me their liege. Basically, he thought I was being self-important.

Now I knew exactly why Fleur had been worried. My "allies" here were nervous I might behave as if I was their liege. These people had lived their lives as independent lords, never explicitly beneath someone else before. Even if they'd surrendered in war, even if they'd been coerced into being almost vassal-like allies to a greater lord, they had lived proudly with the king as their only formal liege.

But then I, an unprecedented character in this land, had become regent, so they viewed my return with suspicion. Wondering if I was going to subjugate them.

Indeed I was.

I'm going to subjugate you and incorporate you into my own forces. If I can't at least do that, I can't fight against the western lords the former king fled to.

A clash between east and west was about to happen in the kingdom. The most powerful lords in the west were united, with the former king Paffus VI as their emblem.

——Looks like you have a mess to clean up, after all. This is just like what Settsu and Harima did.

You experienced this, too, huh? Well, this is what happens when you try to force people to submit.

——Many people rose up against me, by the way. I had trouble with some of them, but I put them down one by one. Foolish bastards who don't know when to and when not to fight can go to hell.

This had all helped me make up my mind.

Forgive me, Altia—but if Brando turns against me, I'm going to fight your husband.

Of course, I would much prefer if that didn't happen, but looking at Brando's eyes, I thought it might be difficult to avoid.

"My brother-in-law, can I please have your answer?" Brando asked again, more forcefully this time. "Of course, we want to fight together with you, but our land is not your land. I would be happy if you could confirm that for us."

This lord's youthful eyes resembled my own. It was not something that said he just wanted to protect his own land; rather, he had the face of a man who yearned to expand more and more if he could. And that was why he couldn't work under me.

My father-in-law Ayles Caltis and his allies also watched my face uneasily.

I raised the palm of my hand to them, as if to explain myself. I didn't act panicked, though. I was the regent, after all. *I'm not like any of you.*

"Fear not, for I shall not covet your lands. In fact, protecting your lands is my duty as His Majesty's regent. We all have him as our only liege." Brando exhaled as if my words had finally placated him, but he was still eyeing me carefully. "Hereafter, I may have to go to war in the name of His Majesty. I would certainly like to have your cooperation at that time."

With that, things calmed down. However, I was now mostly convinced of one thing: At some point, there would be killing between my forces and some of the people here. To unify the realm, I'd have to eliminate some of my former friends.

"Is your wife here today?" I asked.

"Yes. She is looking forward to seeing you. I believe she is being shown around the courtyard at the moment." Brando's expression softened.

"Tell her I'd love to see her."

◇

Altia came up to my room. The rappas were keeping tight surveillance around the perimeter, so even if there was a Naaham spy, they couldn't get all the way in here.

Altia's hair had grown since we'd last met, making her look more feminine.

"You were just a little girl before you were married, and now look at you."

"Well, I'm a young woman now. I've already got a daughter, too," Altia said, giggling. Brando was truly a lucky man to have her as his wife. That's just how highly I'd thought of him.

I talked with Altia for a while about old times. Our memories were not of here but of Nayvil, so it almost felt like a brother-and-sister vacation getaway.

"It feels so strange—you being regent and all the kingdom groveling before you." She laughed as she enjoyed some tea.

"I'll make them grovel even more," I said, and then got serious. "Altia, if at all possible, I want you to convince your husband to bow to me," I implored her. "As regent, I'm in a position of leadership over Brando. I want you to talk to him so he doesn't shirk that responsibility. If he defies me, it won't do him any good."

It was a risky thing to ask. There was always the possibility that Altia would tell Brando about this, putting him on guard. Nevertheless, I asked her because I thought she would do as I said—well, not really.

I didn't want to betray my sister. I at least wanted to speak my mind with her, my blood relative. In the future, I'd undoubtedly be able to trust fewer people than ever before—an inevitable consequence of climbing the social hierarchy.

Altia kept quiet for a moment, but finally she nodded slowly.

"If not for you, I would have died a long time ago. So I want to do as you wish."

It was too soon to feel relieved. Altia wasn't finished.

"But if my husband still tries to defy you…then I'll do what I feel is best. I'm a woman of Naaham now, you know."

She was looking me square in the eye, as if to show she didn't feel bad one bit about what she'd said. I couldn't keep myself from laughing out loud.

"Oh, come on! That's not something to laugh about," Altia pouted, thinking I was making fun of her. Fair enough.

"Sorry, sorry. You really are my sister. You're just like me. If only my brother had a bit more backbone, too."

She stood her ground even in front of the regent. And as someone who'd married into another clan, she'd made the correct response. Altia was fulfilling her duty.

"Altia, I'll be frank with you. I'm going to unify this realm. I'm going to create an age without conflict anywhere in the kingdom."

"That sounds like a dream."

"Being regent is like a dream, too."

Altia nodded a little, as if conceding the point.

"To that end, I need the cooperation of the lords around Fordoneria. Brando is my brother-in-law. If he gives me his all, I'll award him with maybe three prefectures. So…" I put my hand to my chest and said, "No matter what you do, get your husband to submit to me. I'm going to keep on conquering so that you can have confidence in what I said. Ten years from now, I'll be at the top of this kingdom."

Altia got up from her seat. "Your Excellency, thank you very much for your hospitality. I am most honored." She spoke very formally, but soon laughed out loud. "You haven't changed one bit. You're as egotistical and savage as always, but the fact that you're regent means this kingdom's future needed you."

Altia came close and lightly kissed my cheek. For a family member, it was a normal display of affection.

"Please become king. When you do, I don't know what my status will be, or if I'll even be alive, but I think you need to be king. Being under anyone is too restrictive for you."

"Oh, I will."

I stood up as well and hugged Altia tight.

What a ridiculous brother-and-sister conversation. Normal talk just wasn't for us apparently.

"I'm very proud of you, Brother. There's only one problem."

"What problem would that be?"

"You move on women too fast."

That had a lot of punch, coming from my sister...

"Oh, that... You see, with my position, it'd be bad if I didn't have an heir, so... That doesn't exactly mean I'm a womanizer or anything..."

"I wasn't saying you're a womanizer, but the moment you realize a woman is good at something, you fall for her instantly."

How much did she know about this...?

"Miss Kelara for sure. And I can tell from the way you look at one of the vassals you brought with you—something happened with that Yanhaan woman."

"Are you seriously deducing this yourself? You're not spying on me, are you?"

"I just know you really well. You simply weren't in a position to woo women before. Now that you're regent, you can't control yourself."

My sister's observation skills were unbelievable.

"I'll be more careful..." I wasn't sure if I actually could, but that was all I managed to say.

"I also have one other request of you."

"What is it? Whatever it is, don't hold back—though at this point I don't think you would."

"I want to talk with Miss Laviala, too. She was like a sister to me, after all."

© Kaito Shibano

Oh. That's something I can support.

"Actually, she's already here as a bodyguard."

The wardrobe in the room opened with a *squeeeak*. Standing there was Laviala, with tears in her eyes.

"It's so nice to see you again, Lady Altia! Look at how beautiful you've become!" She hugged Altia tightly. Very tightly indeed.

"Miss Laviala, please continue watching over my brother."

"Of course I will! My whole life is dedicated to Lord Alsrod!"

It was strange listening to this right next to them.

"I think he's going to keep getting more wives, but please put up with him."

"Huh? Ah… Yes…I've already given up on that front."

What did she mean by that…?

"Say," I interrupted, "since we're here, why don't we open up a bottle to mark the occasion?"

Afterward, the three of us shared stories and caught up together. I felt like that one room had fully gone back in time.

We'd surely never be able to have such an occasion again. For us all to come together in happiness ten or twenty years from now, it'd take a number of miracles. But we enjoyed the moment so we could forget about such things.

Just for now, let's go back ten years.

Five years to the day after I defeated Orsent Cathedral, I was at war with the remnants of the Santira clan, who had fled to the western part of the kingdom.

The Santiras had formerly been the greatest power in Fortsouth Prefecture, but they had collapsed when I took the royal capital. Their clan head, Leggus Santira, had gone into hiding in Sinju Prefecture to the west of Fortwest.

Naturally, I had arranged to have the fighting end on this auspicious day. We had long since known where they were clinging to existence. I personally didn't need to go into battle, but I might as well be in front.

"Red Bears, White Eagles, follow me! Orcus and Leon, I trust you're ready?"

"O' course!" Orcus Bright shouted, coming to stand on the left of my horse. His arms were bigger than ever, so when he swung his sword it was so fast you couldn't tell if it was a sword or an axe.

"The White Eagles are all warmed up!" From the right came Leon Milcolaia. This elven soldier had an intellectual demeanor, the polar opposite of Orcus. But thanks to that, I often got to hear some bizarre conversations.

"Say, Leon."

"Yes, sir? What is it?"

"I hear you've been fooling around quite a bit with some of the court ladies recently. Is that true?"

"Oh, that's... Well..." Leon was clearly uncomfortable talking about it.

"Guilty as charged, huh? I didn't think you were much into that sort of thing. I'm not going to punish you for something like that. Just don't seduce His Majesty's daughter. She's either twelve or thirteen, right at the age where they're pining for affection."

"My apologies... It's just...when they come on to me, I don't know how to refuse..."

I had a good guess at what this was about. In peacetime, the White Eagles acted as court guards, among other things. The court ladies must have been flirting with him then. Leon was already almost sixty years old, but as an elf, he still had his youthful good looks. Also, as a former mercenary, he'd cheated death on many occasions, so he had a different twinkle in his eye from the neighborhood playboys. The more experienced a person was, the more attractive.

Of course, I was basically the same as far as being youthful. One of my profession's special abilities was Conqueror's Aura. Anyone with this profession aged more slowly while they were in their castle acting as a conqueror, along with the rest of their kin. I was a regent, not a king, but apparently I still benefited from it. I was twenty-eight now, but I hadn't changed at all since taking the royal capital at twenty-three.

"Leon, one reason they come on to you is because you're not married," I told him. "It's about time you started thinking about who's going to succeed the Milcolaia clan."

"Long ago, I was married to a girl in my village, but she passed away. After that...I wandered from place to place as a mercenary, so I haven't remarried..."

I understood the desire not to be tied down, but I'd given all my captains the title of viscount. It wasn't exactly an honorary title, so I would really appreciate it if he took that part seriously.

"Orcus, how many children do you have?" I asked the captain of the Red Bears on the other side of me.

"I got twelve. And my oldest and second-oldest boys are working hard in the Red Bears!"

"See? Orcus has got you beat there."

Leon, who was always pestering Orcus about little things, looked ashamed.

"M-my apologies, sir..."

"You all are lords, too. Get yourself a wife!"

"I do have a number of candidates for adoption, so my clan will continue on..."

"Are you daft? You have all these court ladies in love with you, so pick one of them. As long as they don't have too important a family, I'll make it happen."

"As you wish, sir..."

Orcus laughed at Leon and his weak answer.

"All right, Leon. Get me Leggus Santira's head. Attack their left flank. We'll advance from the other side."

"Yes, sir! To think the clan that once dominated Fortsouth would end its existence commanding only fifteen hundred men... Nothing lasts."

Before I tried to answer, the profession residing in my mind spoke to me.

——**Every generation has a certain number of people who don't understand the trends of the times. Despite having no future aside from following whoever is powerful, they still remain senselessly defiant until death. Naturally, this clan will fall into ruin. I have no idea why they're being so obstinate.**

Still, Oda Nobunaga, it might sometimes be better than people who faithlessly switch lieges at the drop of a hat, right?

——**It depends. If they do it right before they're defeated, you can't trust them, but if they've always misjudged the trends—nay,**

if they don't even try to see the trends, they're simply incompetent. You can't call that fidelity.

I agreed with that. This Leggus Santira person had no foresight, either. If he'd only bowed to me, then I'd have given him at least a tiny plot of land, but he'd always persisted in defying me.

"Leon, get a good look at that Santira bastard's attitude before he dies. We'll know what kind of man he is based on whether he takes it like a warrior or surrenders like a coward."

"Understood. Does that mean you want us to take him alive?"

"If he seems to be begging for his life, bring him here for now."

"As you wish!"

Leon's White Eagles charged the hillock where the enemy lay. The enemy's position during the melee wasn't bad, but they were horribly outnumbered, so a small terrain advantage didn't matter to begin with.

"Let's go, Orcus."

"Time to earn some new medals!"

By now, the Black Dogs must've been attacking from the rear. That was when we were to charge in.

Just before we were about to smash into them, the enemy's right flank broke into chaos. They were beset by a group of hounds, howling and biting them to death.

"Looks like the werewolf attack worked perfectly," I said.

It was Dorbeau's Black Dogs. Their attacks were unwaveringly ferocious, so they were quite handy at times like this.

"This battle is completely over. They might have thought they could still retreat, but now they're entirely cut off."

The enemy was ready to flee. The werewolves in beast form had broken them from behind, and my force was attacking in front. Against their regiment of ten or fifteen hundred, we had only to wait for them to be ground to dust.

"I don't understand what they're trying to do, Your Excellency,"

Orcus said loudly. You had to raise your voice during battle, but he was being loud even for that. "What can they hope to do in a field battle with such pathetic numbers? They'll just all be killed. If they had set up a hard defense in a fort, help mighta come to 'em, and even if they couldn't expect that, they coulda fled away scared or even given themselves over, already tied up."

"So you mean they're being irrational. A certain portion of people are thoughtless creatures like this—even if their lives are at stake."

If all lords fought for their lives with all their might, this era would've been much different. Among those I'd eliminated, half had resisted me without a plan, leading to their deaths.

"Feel free to decimate our foes this time around. Let's go."

"Yessir! Things've been rather peaceful lately, so this is perfect!"

Indeed, these past five years had been an improvement. Nothing resembling a great war had happened—or rather, I hadn't caused one.

I'd fully established our power in the capital vicinity. On the other hand, the former king, who'd fled west, continued to call himself king and was being supported by the most powerful western lords.

"This peacetime will probably fall apart again, though. I think things will be even worse."

"I hope so. If we're not at war, I'll be outta business. That'd be far worse. My life is for killin'!"

I drew my sword, the Stroke of Justice. When I was on horseback, my three-jarg spear would get in the way. Orcus, with his massive sword, charged in as well.

"Get on your knees, you Santira bastards! I, Alsrod Nayvil, have come to slay you by my own hand!"

I thought they'd come for my head upon hearing my voice, but the opposite was true.

"It's the murderous regent!"

"The most powerful man in the realm!"

"Retreat! Retreat!"

Terror came over the enemy soldiers' faces as they attempted to flee. Apparently the rumors about me were getting more and more exaggerated. It was as if the enemy thought I was some sort of invincible demon.

Special ability Conqueror's Presence acquired.
Takes effect when recognized as a conqueror by many at once. All abilities are tripled from the usual.
Additionally, all who lay eyes on you experience either awe or fear.

Special ability Conqueror's Guidance activated.
Allies' trust and focus will double. Additionally, their offensive and defensive abilities improve by thirty percent.

These two abilities were granted by my profession, Oda Nobunaga. I could fight at a level no normal person could ever hope to achieve. Frankly, I didn't feel like I could lose—or rather, there was no way I could lose.

Try as they might, the enemy had nowhere to flee, so they ended up colliding with one another and collapsing. I didn't intend to go to the trouble of killing such second-rate soldiers, but the way they acted made me wonder if their general was even here.

Orcus had already charged into them and was lopping off heads left and right. "Wimps! Babies! Stay off the battlefield if you're not ready for a fight!"

Indeed. Now that they had arrived on the field of war, they should be here to kill, or at least to die. If they didn't want to do either, they shouldn't have come in the first place.

I was having trouble finding anyone to fight. The folks around me killed the enemy before I could, and they were already running away, so it was hard to do anything.

Halfway through, I stopped my horse.

"This is pointless now. We've already won."

Almost simultaneously, voices echoed out from the enemy's left flank.

"We've captured the Santira clan head!"

"Our regent is victorious! Our kingdom is victorious!"

"Is it already over? It doesn't feel like I even fought." Orcus came over, not even hiding his disappointment. It wasn't the expression of a victor, at least.

"What's done is done. That's just how that goes. You won't get anything trying to sell prisoners, either."

Had I been a rural lord, I might've taken prisoners home as laborers, but since people were streaming into the royal capital as well as Maust Castle, there was no shortage of labor.

Just then a man with wolf ears walked up. It was the Black Dogs' captain, Dorbeau, wearing the same mean look on his face he always did. Not in a vulgar way—he had the eyes of someone who had spent lots of time in serious contemplation over how to live. The villainous look he'd once had was long gone. This was a sort of testimony to the life he'd lived; he would likely remain this way until the end of his days.

"We latched on to the people who looked like generals, and we've brought three or so here. What would you like to do with them?"

"I'll take them back with us. Although I suppose I don't need to take them all the way to the capital."

Some members of the Santira clan were brought out before me. With their hands tied behind their backs, they looked absolutely miserable. I saw an old man among them: Leggus Santira.

A few of them begged for mercy. Apparently they were asking for leniency because they were related to so-and-so in the royal court.

"Leon, did they beg for their lives?"

"Yes. They bent the knee of their own accord. They weren't even wounded."

"Very well. Behead them all."

Nobody tried to stop it. They must've decided it was appropriate.

"People of the Santira clan, I'm terribly sorry, but although my army has accepted plenty of capable individuals into its ranks, there will never be openings for the incompetent. They would truly do more harm to my men than any foe, you see."

I had them taken away to the executioner.

Thus, the Santira clan was officially no more. Not everyone can think five or six steps ahead, but not even one? That was a lost cause.

◇

After finishing simple post-battle cleanup, we returned to one of Sinju's towns that was allied to the king and stayed the night. We were quite far from the royal capital, so I was going to take time getting back.

Sinju Prefecture was large, so subjugating all of it was difficult. It had a tendency to be a hotbed of fugitives like Leggus Santira. It was inefficient to send troops there, so I'd been putting it off until after I'd crushed Orsent Cathedral.

I collapsed on the sofa upon entering my room. War caused fatigue to build up from all manner of things. It was a game of life and death, after all. You might think I should just not go to the front line, then, but my presence there raised the whole army's morale, so I had to. Oda Nobunaga was never the type to go out on the front line, so I did think that was a bit odd, but fighting was so fun I didn't care. Just living at court all the time would be too stuffy.

Apparently someone else felt the same way.

"Well done, Lord Alsrod!" Laviala entered the room cheerfully. She had been on the battlefield but not at the front.

"What a relief to be back in battle after so long! Staying in the palace all ladylike just doesn't seem right for me..."

"I thought you'd say that. You've been hard at work on domestic affairs lately, after all."

"Can't we just stay on the offensive all the time, Lord Alsrod?" Laviala made a pouty face. My relationship with Laviala hadn't changed one bit since before I was even a petty lord.

"There's a time for attacking, and there's a time for defending. That's what it means to be regent. If I were constantly at war, His Majesty would wonder what I was doing."

Since I'd defeated Orsent Cathedral, the capital area had been at peace. Or rather, with its defeat the forces against me had disappeared from the capital. That fight had gone as I'd hoped, but it had also shown me that I could get tripped up relying on my forces alone. And so I'd changed my plans to taking control of the royal capital. I'd have to do that sooner or later either way.

I beckoned Laviala onto the sofa and stroked her hair.

"Is it not time to attend to official business yet, Lord Alsrod?" Laviala said, looking more relieved than anything.

"Not while I'm on an expedition. When I'm away, I leave that to Yanhaan. She's capable."

My biggest accomplishment in the past five years had been replacing the bureaucrats with new ones. I'd gathered a great deal of new personnel by using exams.

"The new people really are passionate about their jobs. I often hear that the quality of the bureaucrats has improved."

New didn't quite seem the right way to put it. The first round of people had already been at their jobs for five years.

"The people I brought in are brilliant. Yanhaan is savvy as an apothecary, too. They're not even comparable to those foolish bastards who'd inherited the position purely by privilege."

Laviala buried her face against me. Even after I'd been with her for so long, it was something I never got tired of.

"You sure have driven out a lot of people with their old-fashioned views."

I'd slowly gotten rid of those who held us back to make way for new talent.

"They were guilty of dereliction of duty."

It was somewhat risky to dismiss a bunch of people while I was fighting the cathedral, but once the situation had stabilized, it was nothing to worry about. And there was no risk of them rallying against me when I did it bit by bit.

"Just please make sure you don't arouse His Majesty's suspicions."

"I know. This isn't a power struggle between him and me—I've mostly left his influence alone. I mean, I haven't reformed the government structure at all. He doesn't think anything of it."

No bureaucrats loyal to the current king, Hasse I, would be left anyway, so it hadn't affected his power. There were many sorts of "failed government officials" in the capital vicinity who remained only to do paperwork, regardless of who became king. One by one, I had meticulously replaced those people with my own board pieces. Thanks to that, my power wouldn't be wavering too much, and work wouldn't stack up if I was away from the capital for a bit. I sent anyone who couldn't work as a bureaucrat on the capital front line to somewhere more stable, like Maust. Fanneria was one such person.

It had taken five years, but my ideas were almost always accepted in the capital now. In the meantime, King Hasse now had a virtual web of henchmen, but they didn't have any land, soldiers, or money.

"If only you could just unify the realm, with your power more secure now."

I caught the scent of perfume coming from Laviala's hair; it was an expensive product sourced from a far-off land. So many luxury goods came into the capital. Orsent Cathedral wasn't able to keep them in Fortwest Prefecture as before. This truly was the height of our prosperity.

"The battle is far from over, though. No doubt about it."

"I'm fine with that. For my part, I will protect you, Lord Alsrod, even with my life." Laviala wrapped her arms around me. "That's the only thing I can do that no one else can. I'll probably have more and more rivals anyway…"

I was a bit startled.

"You know I've been refraining from having more affairs lately. Besides, now that I'm married to His Majesty's sister, I can't go on acquiring more concubines."

That was the truth. After Lumie had become my legal wife, I hadn't publicly taken more wives. That was how I'd maintained the peace for five years, so there shouldn't be any issues.

© Kaito Shibano

"I heard a rumor the boy Yanhaan had two years ago is yours."

Of course that rumor was true. Yanhaan and I were lovers, through and through. I was the one who'd felt attracted to her while we were performing tea ceremony together. I'd also taken an interest due to her success as a solo businesswoman. She had different values from the other lords' daughters, so, frankly, she was simply interesting.

I'd offered to take custody, but Yanhaan had said she wanted the boy to be her own heir. Apparently she had come over to this realm on her own, unmarried, so that was the perfect choice to make.

"Even if you haven't made them concubines, you've had a few lovers, haven't you?" The suspicion in Laviala's voice stung.

"It's been five years—temptation happens."

I realized my words carried no confidence.

As a big sister, did Laviala see me as a promiscuous little brother now?

Just then there was a knock at the door. The sound alone gave me a fairly good idea of who was on the other side.

"I'm sorry, Laviala. These are still working hours, so anyone can come in."

Laviala quickly straightened up, though she seemed a bit unsatisfied.

When I opened the door, Kelara was standing there.

"The tentative plans for the invasion of the Northlands are finished, so I brought them over."

"Good work, but you shouldn't bring that here when I'm on an expedition."

Her timing was a bit unfortunate. Laviala looked like she felt we'd had our date interrupted.

"You told me to bring it right away once it was finished."

"You're right, sorry. Give it here. Laviala is here, too, so that's perfect. Let's discuss it for a bit."

Those plans were, plainly speaking, to subjugate the northern lords who had yet to bend the knee to me. Naturally, the plans were ostensibly to subjugate the lords not bowing to the king.

At the moment, the regions not under the king's authority could be divided into two main areas. One was the Westlands. This was where the former king, Paffus VI, had fled to, so it represented a powerful enemy. Of course, the Westlands weren't totally united to begin with.

The Westlands were in an internal conflict for supremacy. Outwardly they had Paffus VI as their king, but quarrels remained.

On the other hand, the Northlands were so far away from the royal capital, they always tended to be culturally backward. Perhaps that was why they were still at the stage before unification by a small number of powerful lords; instead, minor powers were crawling everywhere like ants swarming on candy.

"The plan is to first take out the Margrave of Machaal in Machaal Prefecture. I don't know if he'll surrender right away or if he'll resist to the end. Still, if we take them out, the petty lords will be sure to give themselves up."

"I believe that is not a bad plan," Kelara replied without so much as a smile. No one would guess she was my lover from her stoic demeanor.

"Umm…I have a very simple question… Do you mind?" Laviala raised her hand. "Sequentially speaking, shouldn't we be attacking the powerful enemies in the Westlands?" she asked. "The lords of the Northlands are farther away, for one, and they're not particularly a threat, either…"

"That is true. I can see your point as well, Lady Laviala. The greater danger is in the west, where they're supporting the former king."

Apparently Kelara's relaxed attitude had further annoyed Laviala, who looked a bit put off. This was a compatibility problem. Kelara was a female officer with the distinct air of a royal capital native.

"Your face tells me you already knew that, Miss Kelara," said Laviala. "*Sigh*… I always feel like I'm getting left behind."

"Not at all, Lady Laviala. You are a remarkable individual, and I believe His Excellency loves you very much. At the very least, more than he loves me."

What a caveat. I didn't remember saying anything like that.

"Th-that's true…," said Laviala. "I do have a feeling Lord Alsrod visits my room far more…"

It's not a competition! Think of how awkward this is for me!

"Yes, I…do wish I could talk with His Excellency more at night, but I have a cold personality, so maybe he's avoiding me."

True, Kelara wasn't exactly warm and friendly, but these words clearly had thorns. I'd thought Kelara wasn't the type to worry about such things, but apparently that had changed, too, over time...

"Kelara, that's the first I've heard."

"I didn't think it was worth mentioning. Let's continue with the plan. May I go first? If there are any mistakes, please correct me."

"All right. Go ahead..."

Kelara spread out a map she'd brought with her and proceeded to point to various spots with a rod.

"We will advance from Maust Castle like so."

"Right," Laviala said. "That makes sense given our path. But I still don't know the answer to my question."

Yes, that still didn't answer why we were attacking the Northlands lords. Kelara then smoothly moved her rod to a lord near Maust Castle.

"It is possible this will cause Ayles Caltis, Marquess of Brantaar, and Brando Naaham, Count of Olbia, to raise their armies."

As my sister's husband, Brando had received the rank of count and the title of Count of Olbia four years ago.

"No, would they really...?" Laviala scowled. I had told her such a conflict might happen someday, but she probably hadn't really thought about when.

"That's what this is about. The real enemy is people relatively close to my domain capital, who deep down don't fully submit to me. These guys will think of trying to get rid of me when they get the chance. While they think of me as an ally, they don't want to be beneath me in the end."

"So you mean if there's going to be a big rebellion while you're attacking the Westlands anyway, you'd rather attack the Northlands first to draw them out? Because it would be a safer war in terms of scale?"

Sure enough, Laviala was pretty smart herself. She could assess the situation very quickly.

"Of course, this is a supposition, presuming the *worst-case scenario*. If His Excellency's in-laws don't start a rebellion, then that is a happy outcome in itself."

"No one would openly steal gold coins from a table in a crowd. But if there were no onlookers present, some people would stealthily swipe the coins. In a word, I'm going to test my in-laws—tell them, *If you're going to kill me, now's your chance.*"

I knew from my rappas that my in-laws almost certainly didn't think well of me. That didn't mean they'd start a rebellion, though. Surely most lieges hadn't gained the total confidence of their subordinates. It might've been more common that their subordinates served them without liking them. Thus, I didn't know unless I tested them.

"I understand what you're saying. However, if they killed Lord Alsrod now, that area would fall into total chaos. I can't imagine it would do them much good."

"Well, not everyone thinks that much about the future, you know."

I intended to build a new era, but even people without the same mettle could get in my way.

◇

Having destroyed the Santiras, I returned to the royal capital. I didn't quite receive a hero's welcome, but it was a nice welcome nonetheless. Upon my return, I went immediately to His Majesty King Hasse I to exchange victory greetings. I didn't want to make him think I was slighting him by any means.

Hasse I may have been thickheaded, but he had ruled for some time now, so his attitude was more kingly than before. Not all the kings in the Kingdom of Therwil's long history had been competent. The bureaucracy was in order well enough to be capable, even if it wasn't outstanding.

"The kingdom is one step closer to unification, thanks to you. Let us keep pushing on together as brothers." Hasse said *brothers* because I was married to his little sister, making us brothers-in-law. "You are still in your twenties. If we continue to remake this realm together over the next ten or twenty years, unification will certainly come someday."

"Indeed. Although this is just my hope…I would like to fully unify all our lands in about five years."

Back when things had calmed down after we took the capital, I had hoped unification would happen in roughly a decade. This was the midway point, in other words.

"Five years, eh? I will certainly look forward to it. The people can call me the Restorer. I like the sound of that," Hasse said profoundly. There was a thin line between becoming a restorer and becoming the last monarch of the Kingdom of Therwil. Of course, this king didn't seem to have many suspicions about the latter. It would be perfect if I could continue deceiving him to the end.

I had essentially used these five years to gain his trust. Power gradually converged on whoever commanded the army when the army was constantly getting sent out to war. Of course, there was a chance that might lead him to worry about giving me too much freedom. As a matter of fact, plenty of people in the past had gained enough power through repeated victories that they could secede from the king or even oust him.

However, doing that too early in the game would only lead to regional power in the capital area, as no matter how much justification he had, lords far away would see the new king as a simple usurper. It would be impossible to maintain enough power to subjugate the entire realm. And then, at some point, he'd be defeated by some foe and have to flee from the central area to the countryside, only to be killed somewhere—this was one way things often went. Thus, it was the right decision to work with the king toward unification, for now.

Yes, Oda Nobunaga was saying it, too.

——Are you listening? Make use of upper authorities while you can. Ashikaga Yoshiaki was a pain to deal with, but I never killed him. Truthfully, I didn't quite want to exile him, as that's enough trouble as it is… I even suggested we make his son the next shogun, but he refused…

*   *   *

I know. I don't intend to make the same mistakes as you.

——I don't appreciate your tone, Alsrod. I don't remember ever mishandling Yoshiaki. Until I became more powerful than him, I never once totally vanquished him.

Even so, there was an alliance against you, right? So you were in some ugly situations. I don't feel like making more enemies than I have to.

Oda Nobunaga cackled. The reverberations inside my head were rather annoying.

——Liar. At your core you can't get enough of war. You're even sending troops to the Northlands because you want to fight against your own kinsmen, right? You want to cross swords with everyone who can fight.

It was hard to say for sure. Maybe I couldn't totally deny it.

You might say Mineria's leader, Ayles Caltis, was the first general I'd admired, as well as the first wall I'd come up against. As the Nayvil clan had been on the brink of collapse, I'd awoken to my power.

Ayles Caltis must have been around his midforties by now. Left alone, he would weaken both physically and mentally. I...did actually have a desire to fight him before then.

——Do as you like. Your wife might hate you from the bottom of her heart, or she might surprisingly say nothing—it's difficult to tell.

Oda Nobunaga had defeated his own father-in-law in a siege, so he seemed to be somewhat sentimental about this sort of thing. Of course, he'd banished the son of the man who'd killed his father-in-law, so there wouldn't have been any problem morally speaking.

My post-victory report continued.

"Also, Sir Regent, I have a question," the king said a bit hesitantly.

"Yes, what is it?"

"Are you getting along with Lumie? As her brother, I wonder about her. And she got married as a naive thirteen-year-old, so I thought misunderstandings might abound..."

Ahh, so he was wondering about that. In a sense, the king might've been more at liberty to worry about his sister now. When I'd first met him, he'd had nothing, and he had been thinking only about becoming king. Once one's basic needs are met, he can concern himself with greater matters beyond himself.

As I could give him a favorable answer about this, I was relieved myself.

"Well, then, allow me to speak frankly." I put on a solemn face.

"S-sure..."

"When we were first married, she still was somewhat childish, but now that over five years have passed—to be honest, I never imagined she would become this beautiful. Perhaps her royal blood is to thank."

Hasse looked relieved. Just then, someone slipped out from behind the curtains. I didn't sense hostility, so it wasn't even frightening. I'd already known someone was there.

"Ah, it so pleases me to hear that. My heart was racing." Lumie showed herself. She put her hand to her breast in relief, and indeed they were big enough to call breasts now. I'd never thought they'd grow this much...

Some court poet or someone had said she was now the most beautiful woman in the capital, and they weren't wrong. With age she had naturally become more beautiful, and intermingled was the gleam of intelligence together with her inborn kindness. She might truly be the ideal princess. Her hiding-in-curtains habit hadn't changed, however.

"Don't be bothering His Majesty too much, Lumie."

"Oh? But you said you have to do whatever you can to win in war." When she laughed like that, she seemed a bit like the little girl she had been when we first met.

Damn—this was supposed to be a political marriage, but I've really fallen for her. Seraphina would get a kick out of this.

◇

After spending some time with Lumie, that night I went to Seraphina's quarters. When I'd first met Seraphina, she must've been fifteen or sixteen. Several years had passed since then, but she didn't look any different.

That was because of my profession, Oda Nobunaga. All my wives stayed gorgeous for me. I really had to thank him for this.

"Oh, you want to be with me? Shouldn't you spend the night with your proper wife?" Seraphina giggled at me from her chair. Her indomitable attitude never changed.

But Seraphina must've had a good idea of why I was here.

"I'm going to fight to unify this realm, Seraphina. I'm sure you understand that, too."

"Of course I do. You know I told you when we got married I wanted to be with a man who would be king."

Seraphina came over and leaned against me. Her tendency to test me with suggestive eyes hadn't changed, either.

"If your family and clan had to be destroyed for that to happen, would you be able to accept it?" I asked, separating my body from hers a bit. "Your father might rebel against me, and when that happens, I plan to take him on full force. Not knowing when Brantaar might betray me will jeopardize my future plans. Especially when it's my father-in-law, others might secede as well."

Seraphina's face turned somewhat grim. She didn't say anything immediately. I waited patiently. No matter her answer, what I had to do was already decided.

Faint tears welled up in her eyes.

"How strange. Before, I thought I didn't care what I sacrificed if only you were king, but now that it's my reality, I'm so afraid. I wonder if everyone I know might die…"

I said nothing, silently hugging Seraphina close. I knew that was the most I could do. Unfortunately, no matter how much it saddened her, I couldn't let up on how I treated any rebels who appeared. And so all I could do was be silent.

Seraphina must've cried on me for some time. I'd known she was delicate, but she sure felt light. She seemed like she might melt away like candy.

"This is all assuming he takes up arms against me, of course. I swear to you I would never do such a thing as kill him on suspicion of treason."

If I did that, even people who obeyed me would lose their trust in me. After that would come a hell in which no one would follow me. It was definitely a better idea to guarantee that you'd protect anyone who obeyed you.

"No, I'm sure my family will attack you. They're not flexible enough to accept the new world you're making, darling."

Seraphina went over to a locked cosmetics box in the room. What she retrieved wasn't cosmetics but, oddly, a letter.

"Read this, darling."

I immediately took a look at the letter she passed me.

"It says he wants to show me hospitality in his home and that you should come along."

"*Hospitality* is a code word in the Caltis clan," said Seraphina. "It means 'destroy.' It's a little trick to reduce risk should it be found."

So he'd been slipping it into what appeared to be trivial family communications. When it was mentioned among a multitude of other topics, nobody would notice.

"I've got several letters urging me to send info, too. I think he really does mean to do it."

"Thanks for telling me. You really do understand me better than anyone."

I kissed Seraphina on the lips. Then, perhaps having made up her mind, she sat in the chair.

"Actually, I know the answer, but I'll ask you anyway," she told me.

"Sure, as you like. You have the right to do that."

I was certain she'd ask me not to attack her family or to spare their lives. But that was naive of me. I'd forgotten Seraphina was a much more passionate person than that.

"Kill me for treason," Seraphina said with a smile. "Then you'll be able to attack the Caltis clan without any reserve. If I'm here, your judgment might be compromised." Apparently Seraphina had thought of this as a way to resolve her conflicting emotions.

I sighed and forced a smile. I couldn't feel angry.

"What is your profession?"

"Um, Saint…"

It raised luck by 30 percent for people close to her—that was what a Saint's ability was supposed to be.

"Exactly. You are a saint to me. A person who kills the saint protecting them is a hopeless fool. I don't intend to live so foolishly. You only get one life, after all."

"You won't even divorce me and send me away…?"

"I'm not foolish enough to divorce a person as enchanting as you. I want to keep you as my own."

I wondered why I was seriously trying to cajole my own wife, but it was quite true that I didn't want to lose her.

"If I were your only wife, that would be a convincing argument."

"You're the one who brought me a concubine so that I could build more alliances. I'm grateful to you for setting me up with Fleur. You're also the one who was so enthusiastic about me marrying Lumie."

The tension had relaxed enough for me to make such quips. Also, Seraphina had given me an idea.

"Seraphina, I am sorry to bring this up now, but I want to take another wife."

"Of course. Who did you have in mind? You know I'm open to these things."

"Soltis Nistonia's daughter should be of age now."

Before my big military operation, I wanted to pave the way just a bit more. Soltis Nistonia was a powerful lord in Siala Prefecture who'd helped me as I'd expanded my influence along the coast. After the Antoini clan—who'd been ruling most of the prefecture—lost to me, he had become the greatest power in Siala. Furthermore, the other day I'd received news that the vagabond head of the Antoinis had died of illness, essentially snuffing the clan from existence.

Economically, lords holding seaports far outstripped landlocked lords with the same land area. Letting him control all of Siala would represent a risk of betrayal, so I hadn't done that, but it certainly was a golden age for the Nistonias now.

I'd actually met Soltis's daughter, Yuca, once before, back when I'd invited his family to Maust Castle in order to form an alliance. In case they were killed at the castle, he had left his son back home and come with the rest of his family. Among them was Yuca.

Several years had passed since then, so Yuca must be in her midteens. She was still unmarried, perhaps because my power had covered the surrounding area, meaning they hadn't really needed to think about cooperating with other lords.

I wanted to also be able to transport troops and supplies by sea in the upcoming war. To that end, I wanted to reaffirm my ties with the Nistonias, especially since they had originally ruled in that area, making them my conquered vassals. The more insurance against betrayal the better.

After listening to what I had to say, Seraphina asked, "So do people say this Yuca girl is beautiful?"

"No such rumors have reached my ears. If you're in doubt, look into it yourself."

◇

I first invited Soltis to the royal capital in order to discuss the marriage. My pretext was that because he was still a viscount, he should come to receive the rank of count.

I convinced the king to allow the investiture right away. Soltis thereupon became the Count of Siala.

After the celebratory banquet, I summoned him to an empty room and had the conversation. I called Seraphina, Fleur, and Kelara to entertain him. I hadn't invited Laviala on this occasion, but she came anyway. Apparently Lumie was playing with my kids.

"…And so I would like to have your daughter as a wife. I'd have trouble answering if you asked why I have so many wives… But just think of it as serving the relationships of the respective clans. My own daughters and son are still too young anyway."

"You're so lusty, you can't get enough women, right, darling?" said Seraphina—it was hard to tell if she meant it or if it was a joke. She must've at least half meant it.

On the other hand, Fleur was calmly refilling Soltis's cup.

"Perhaps this is not my place, but currently it would make little difference to your relationships with nearby lords whether you married your daughter to them or not. That being the case, marrying her to His Excellency would not be a bad option, I think."

Fleur always did things logically, in all likelihood because of her efforts to keep the smallish Wouge clan alive. Small- to medium-sized clans quickly got destroyed when they didn't think of the consequences of their actions. A single mistake would lead to instant destruction.

"Well…I am very honored by the proposal itself…but there is something that worries me for a completely different reason…"

Soltis was starting to get some gray hairs, but he still served as the Nistonia clan head. His son wasn't old enough to inherit all authority yet.

"Good gracious, what could that be?" Fleur asked without smiling. I'd brought Fleur here because no one was as good as her at getting down to the point. She was much more useful than some unskilled bureaucrat.

Laviala, incidentally, was sitting there purely to watch. No matter how much she'd tried, she had always had a simple honesty to her—or to phrase it another way, her rural habits never went away. To a born-and-bred denizen of the royal capital, all of us besides Kelara were country bumpkins.

"Well…this is embarrassing to say…but seeing Your Excellency's wives' faces, my daughter is completely outclassed—or rather…"

Judging from Soltis's expression, he didn't seem to be joking at all.

"I haven't yet transferred clan headship to my son, but he is already married, and I even have grandchildren. So there is no worry about the continuation of the clan, but because of that, when thinking of my daughter's happiness, I want her to be married to a husband who will love her."

"I see," said Fleur. "You mean to say you don't want your daughter to become His Excellency's concubine in name only. You wish for better for her."

Soltis answered Fleur with a bashful "That is correct."

I hadn't expected to feel the way I did. I could very clearly tell Soltis genuinely wished for his family's happiness—that itself wasn't strange at all. In fact, it was utterly natural. I, however, had long since set such feelings aside. Perhaps I hadn't really forgotten it, but I also hadn't given that sort of thing very much thought.

I wondered if I'd feel that way when my children came of age. Or would the slow aging from my Oda Nobunaga profession make me always feel the same way I did now?

I wasn't sure how to respond. To be sure, I was quite blessed in terms of wives. Laviala, who had always treated me as a little brother, as well as Seraphina and Fleur—they were all truly beautiful. Lumie had grown to look absolutely angelic, and my lovers Kelara, Yanhaan, and Yadoriggy all had their own different attractive qualities.

At this point, if I were asked if I could love an unremarkable girl if I took her as a concubine, I wasn't entirely sure. If word got to Soltis that I was being neglectful of his daughter, giving him a bad impression of me, it sure as hell would defeat the purpose.

"I see," Fleur said. "I think that is a natural concern to have. Well, would you please let us meet with your daughter once? I will show her around the royal capital, just as we showed her around the castle in Maust."

Soltis agreed. After he left the room, Kelara asked me, "Will you postpone the Northlands invasion?"

"It won't be long from now."

◇

Soltis's daughter, Yuca, came to the royal capital sooner than I'd expected—twelve days after my meeting with Soltis. He must've sent a horseback messenger to his territory right away, not wanting us to think he was hesitant. He may have gone to some unnecessary trouble because of us.

Unsure how to feel about meeting Yuca, I decided to quiet my mind with Yanhaan's tea ceremony. As a matter of fact, I'd had a tea ceremony room built within the royal palace; it was a pain to visit Yanhaan's residence every time. Because of my position, I had to be careful of assassins and such anyway.

As we partook of our tea, we didn't speak more than was necessary. Tea ceremony was a time-honored ritual in which mundane hierarchical relationships disappeared.

I slowly drank all the dark-green tea. Today's tea seemed just a bit bitter, but maybe it was only reflecting my mental state.

"You seem troubled. I can tell just by looking at you," Yanhaan remarked as I finished drinking.

Guru is a word that perfectly described Yanhaan's face during tea ceremony. She was both dignified and benevolent, as if to say, *I am the master of this art.* It didn't at all seem like the look of a person who had built a fortune in business.

"I'm going to meet with Soltis's daughter. Seems it'll be an interview, so it's got me distracted."

We'd finished our tea, so it didn't matter if we discussed something here now.

"Astray and in doubt every time, no matter how many times you've gone through it—that is love."

"In conventional wisdom, sure, but I never thought I'd feel this way myself. I want to hear what you think."

Yanhaan narrowed her eyes a bit and showed a faint smile. She was outstanding as a bureaucrat, as well, but her expression now was totally unbureaucratic.

"If it seems to be an intervieeew, then why don't you try to act as you would for one?" Yanhaan answered slowly. "If that is what your heart says, I think you ought to take things as they come instead of resisting. What are your thoughts on the matter? There are nooo correct answers when it comes to love anyway. The more you try to find them, the more you will fail."

Those words fell heavily onto my heart.

"All right. I'll try doing that."

"Indeed, sir. You are human, too, Your Excellency," Yanhaan said, smiling.

◇

It was time to meet Yuca, and she would come into the room where I was waiting. I had Kelara there also, as Yuca might get nervous if it suddenly became one-on-one.

Finally, the door opened. I gulped. Which of us would be more nervous?

I tried to see what she looked like, but I couldn't see her face. She was shielding it from view with her hands. I thought she looked somewhat like a captured criminal.

"S-sorry… I'm not used to this sort of thing…"

"Nobody is. Why don't you try taking a deep breath?" Kelara gave her pertinent advice.

Yuca really did take a deep breath, and then she removed her hands from her face. I was struck by her rare blue hair, and her eyes were similarly blue. Part of her seemed almost doll-like, but she certainly wasn't unattractive at all. She was quite a graceful young lady.

"You have beautiful hair," I remarked, and then wondered if that was too dull a compliment to give.

"...One of my ancestors fell in love with a merchant's daughter in another continent, so I hear...which is why it's this color..."

"The Nistonia clan does rule the seas, after all. That has to happen sooner or later."

"Yes... I'm very nervous... It feels as though my heart might leap out of my chest."

Her trembling wasn't simply adorable; it made me want to care for her.

"Miss Yuca, please have a seat. I'll fetch you some tea. What would you like?" Kelara waited on her for me.

Afterward, I asked Yuca several questions about herself. She said she wasn't very strong-bodied, so she had almost never played outside or done anything physical. And so, she said, going to Maust when she was young had been a novel experience.

To be frank, I got the impression this young girl really didn't know much about the world. The women I'd met up till now had had the strength to forge their own destinies, but Yuca didn't have such a will to take charge.

That said, I knew Yuca's disposition was typical of a noblewoman. Men and women alike usually considered an indomitable spirit like Seraphina's unladylike, and certain qualities developed only in someone like Fleur, who had carried the fate of her entire clan on her shoulders.

This Yuca girl was the result of a completely normal, loving upbringing. Now, as was a noblewoman's lot in life, she would become a political tool.

In that sense, I hadn't had a normal romance myself.

A normal romance, eh? That might not be so bad.

"So, Miss Yuca, do you have any dreams or aspirations?"

I tried asking her a variety of questions in interview form. I did my best to cast my position as regent from my mind, as that really would make it hard to have a normal romance.

"Dreams? Umm..." She continued to dither as she racked her brain. If I'd asked Seraphina, she would've immediately answered with something ambitious like wanting to be a monarch.

"Miss Yuca, if nothing comes to mind, please don't strain yourself," Kelara gently told her as if she were Yuca's longtime servant.

"Oh right, I remember now. I do have this one dream." Yuca seemed to have come up with something. "I want to have and raise a healthy child."

That certainly wasn't an answer I had been expecting, and Kelara looked puzzled as well.

"Why do you say that?" If I didn't know, I had to ask. That was how you conducted an interview.

"Well, I'm...a very ordinary person, you see... Ah, I'm not trying to be self-deprecating; I simply think it must be the truth. With both of you in front of me, I can tell you live in a different world than I do..." Yuca glanced at Kelara and me and then looked down.

"I've never thought I was a particularly outstanding person," Kelara said with a straight face. I thought that might actually make Yuca feel worse. Kelara was very well-mannered, but she often underestimated herself.

"I've never done anything heroic, nor am I particularly clever... I'm truly just a lord's daughter. Every time I heard about Lady Seraphina or Lady Fleur, I thought they were such strong individuals." Yuca spoke without confidence, but it was very clear she was doing her best to express her honest feelings. "But I couldn't possibly accomplish the sorts of things they have. And my body is feeble, too. I have only learned a minimum of etiquette at the castle; I truly have nothing else. They say a lady is her clan's diplomat, but I don't think I would be well suited to that, either..." Yuca became more and more pessimistic as she spoke. It must've been this girl's personality.

"So with that being the case," she continued, "I would like to leave it to my children." Yuca lifted her head slightly. "I can't be an extraordinary person myself, but maybe I could raise my children as heroes. I think then there would be meaning in my life. Besides, I can teach them about weakness, so perhaps that would in turn help me raise them to be strong…" Just then, Yuca's face brightened, like a flower bursting into bloom.

Her dream was undoubtedly abounding with a mother's love. Her smile was genuinely attractive and simultaneously very reassuring.

Had I been born a lowly commoner and stayed that way, I probably would have wanted to spend my life together with a wife like this.

Of course, Yuca was ordinary only in regard to her skill set; if anyone said her looks were ordinary, the gods would smite them. She was endowed with enough beauty and kindness that she could be used in a religious mural with no embellishment necessary.

I want to make this girl happy, I thought, as if by reflex. No, there was still something haughty and regent-like remaining there. *I want to be happy with this girl.* Then, if we could have a relationship where we could laugh together at the little things, maybe my heart could be at ease.

"That is a very selfless and wonderful dream to have," Kelara complimented her in a sort of interviewer-like way.

"No, it's also perfectly selfish." Yuca instantly turned the compliment on its head. "My body is quite frail, so I'm not confident I can have children or even live long enough to raise them. So my dream includes the hope I can watch over them until they're grown." Yuca's poignant smile just then made her look all the more doll-like. In fact, it even seemed like she was an expensive doll someone had made in her likeness.

——What an utterly helpless woman.

Hey, don't add your commentary at a time like this. You're totally out of place here.

——**She does, however, have a certain indefinable charm. Sometimes it's nice to have a woman like her around.**

I agree. I knew my profession would see it my way.

She knew she was weak—she probably knew it so well it made her angry. Looking at it another way, that was a great strength. People who knew they were weak didn't make great mistakes. They were much stronger and smarter than people who mistakenly believed they were strong.

"I-is that answer acceptable...? I'm sorry to speak of something so uninteresting..." Yuca's expression turned timid once again.

"No, that was very interesting. I think Kelara here would say the same."

"Yes. I believe I have a lot to improve on myself. I must be more diligent." She wasn't smiling, but she was surely speaking from the heart. Kelara must've thought it was refreshing, as I did. Yuca had lived in a different world from us military officers.

"We will get in touch with your father again soon. Thank you for coming today."

"Ah, certainly... Er, Your Excellency..." As she stood up, Yuca looked in my eyes in an anxious, pleading sort of way. "I don't think you will be able to make a pathetic woman like me your lover...but please, do not forsake my father and the Nistonia clan..."

She was awfully hunched over, so even though it was probably not something to laugh at, I felt like I was about to.

"You needn't worry. I would never forsake a lord who is loyal to this kingdom."

After she left, I spoke with Kelara about our impressions.

"What do you think? Be honest; I won't get upset."

"I think that young lady would have found happiness a bit more easily had she not been born into an age of war."

"After you spent all that time wandering with His Majesty, I shouldn't be surprised you'd say that."

People unfit for conflict would be born even in times of war. They were usually sacrifices to the violence.

"I didn't see her as just some weakling, though—so I'd like to try bringing her happiness in my own way."

Kelara nodded slowly. "Well, I didn't think Your Excellency would scrap the marriage discussions anyway."

"Wait... You're trying to call me a womanizer, aren't you...?" I felt like I was perfectly faithful to my wives. "At the least, I haven't ever made you unhappy...right?"

"N-no...," Kelara said, a bit bashfully. "Recently, I did wish you would lust after me a little more, but that would upset the balance, wouldn't it?"

More and more I realized Kelara was surprisingly possessive.

◇

I immediately notified Soltis Nistonia that I wanted to take his daughter as a concubine. He seemed somewhat incredulous, taking the trouble to come verify it with me.

"Is such a girl good enough for you...? If you just want to pin down the Nistonia clan, you need not marry her if you don't want to. I won't think anything of it if you decline..."

"No, I'm in love with her from the bottom of my heart. Please do not worry. I also don't intend to choose a wife out of obligation. My only concern is her frailty, but that can't be helped. Instead of making priests pray for her, I'll pray all I can myself."

I now had a good idea of why Soltis had been worried. He would feel sorry for her if she were spent on just a loveless political marriage. In that case he'd rather let her build a nice family with another man, even if he didn't have much power.

"My dear count, I truly do care for her. I'll make her as happy as I am able. Don't think this is just a formality," I declared plainly, my expression serious.

When Yuca came to me, however, she also still looked unconvinced. "Am I good enough for you…?" she asked me, just as her father had.

"You don't realize what charm you have. If you degrade yourself any more, you'll be insulting the man who chose you."

"Ahh…I'm sorry… I just couldn't believe someone like me could become Your Excellency's concubine…"

Yuca had been nervous for some time, so I had to reassure her, stroking the stiffness out of her body.

Later that day, Seraphina let me in on a secret: "Men are fascinated by women they've never experienced before. Just like an epicure." That was a hell of a way to put it, but maybe she wasn't so far off the mark.

"You're awfully savvy," I said to her. "Even if there were a woman just like you, I don't think she could compete."

"With my sass, you mean?"

I'd probably never have this kind of exchange with Yuca, but that didn't bother me. Everyone had their strong suits.

"Well," Seraphina said, "we should take some time to show your new concubine around Maust Castle again."

"Sure, but I'm especially busy lately, so I don't have the time. I don't even have the time to play with my kids."

Indeed, with my closer ties to the Nistonias, I would now finally get the Northlands operation underway. If it succeeded, half of the realm would be mine.

◇

I gathered my army to Maust Castle, and I finally sent them northward in early summer. I had old Commander Kivik look after Maust Castle in my absence. He was eloquent and not at all senile, but with his age his legs and back were getting worn out. His beard and hair were completely white; he even seemed like a deity enshrined in a temple.

"When Kivik dies, I want to give him a grand funeral and burial, but he just doesn't die."

"Lord Alsrod, how disrespectful," Laviala admonished. "But it is true that if he lives too long, it'll be time for his grandchildren to take the reins, which might be hard for his son Mr. Little Kivik."

"You said essentially the same thing I did."

Kivik had helped me do great things for so long, but I couldn't send him to the front lines at his age. This was probably the first big job I'd had for him since I'd let him lead my troops into the capital the first time.

"How is that going for you, Little Kivik?" I asked him as we marched. I called him "Little," but he was older than I. He must've been almost forty.

"I need to ease my father's mind by making a name for myself as soon as possible."

Little Kivik was more of an average person than Kivik; he didn't have a warrior's spirit. Just like his father, though, he had long served me, even if he hadn't garnered as much attention doing so. As far as time of service, the Kivik family would come second only after Laviala.

"Don't worry. Even after you do, Kivik isn't going to want to retire. He won't be satisfied unless he's running around in battle all his life."

"I'm sure he will, but then he will undoubtedly end up dying in battle."

"Nevertheless, he must be over seventy years old by now. At that age, it might be best to let him die in whatever way he likes. I'm sure he won't have any grudges against us then."

"Your Excellency, it's not a joke from the clan's—" Little Kivik's words stopped there, probably because I didn't look like I was joking.

"Little Kivik, I know your father is infirm, but I'm not saying he's less able to command." I needed to make Little Kivik understand that very clearly. "Why would I entrust my castle to a nobody? Do you think it's just an honorary post?"

"No, certainly not... All the more so because it may be the scene of battle, in the worst-case scenario..."

"And that's what this is about. I'm giving him an important job in which it doesn't matter if he is immobile. Now give me your best effort as well."

"Yes, sir!" Little Kivik shouted, seeming ashamed.

He wasn't as capable as his father, but the man was more youthful than he looked. He might have more glory days ahead of him.

All the people of the Kivik clan might come to have a big role in protecting the Nayvil clan if they made great contributions in the wars to come.

"By the way, how old is your son?" I asked Little Kivik.

"My heir is thirteen years old."

"So just about old enough to go to battle, huh?"

"I'm afraid he is quite timid."

Beside me, Laviala said, "Having a little timidity is more reassuring," as if to caution me.

I suppose I do go out on the front lines too much...

"True, but this sort of thing really gets my blood pumping."

As we advanced on the Northlands, the farther north we went, the more fired up I became.

The region colloquially termed the Northlands had a set of prefectures lining both its east and west sides. Word was that originally foreigners from another continent had immigrated there. The allotment of its prefectures was not as convoluted as in the capital area.

Among them, I would first attack the Margrave of Machaal, in Machaal Prefecture, also known as the Gate to the North. The Machaal clan had originally ruled only the southern half of Machaal Prefecture, but eventually they'd subjugated the lords in the north and also extended their domain into part of Misroux Prefecture to the west—they were a great power.

Most notably, the margrave was connected with the former king and his line and had received the title of Count of Misroux. That in itself was justification for the Machaals to subjugate Misroux, and although not all the lords there had submitted to them, they were undeniably the most powerful force in the Northlands.

Additionally, the fact that they were friendly to the former king meant that they were opposed to the current king, Hasse I. Being so far away, there was no direct relationship, but Machaal hadn't sent a messenger to the capital to submit, at least.

Before the offensive, I held a meeting with my top vassals inside a fort. Everyone was gathered around the map. I couldn't relax in my small chair, so I stood. All the captains of my guard troops were present, as well as Laviala, Noen Rowd, Fleur's brother Meissel Wouge, Little Kivik, Kelara Hilara, and more. As a general rule, I didn't bring kingdom officials to the battlefield, so these formed the basis of my military. That meant I hadn't made many calls for troops to the region we marched through.

"Your Excellency, perhaps you should have mobilized troops on a larger scale than this? Of course, I do think we can win, but people might consider this to be the private war of a single lord, rather than a war between the kingdom and its rebels," commented Noen Rowd. He might be middle-aged, but the man was young at heart.

"True, maybe I should've taken more advantage of my position as regent. But I thought it would be a bigger problem to lower the quality of my soldiers by mixing in unmotivated ones. The enemy lords don't exactly do battle relying on numbers alone, either. The Northlands is famous for its cavalry—and they're going to be charging us."

A vicious cavalry attack was all it would take to make a rabble of weak, frightened soldiers rout. If the frontline troops fled, those behind them would also crumble, and that would be the end.

"Nevertheless, as your kin, should not Ayles Caltis and Brando Naaham have joined the war at least...?" After mentioning their names, Noen's voice softened. He must have wondered if it was all right to bring them up.

"I did tell them about it, but they both said they had uprisings in their domains that they needed to suppress."

If they'd claimed to be sick, they'd be told to get replacements, after all. That they had another military operation in progress wasn't as bad an excuse.

"Besides, Noen, a war council isn't for talking about the past. That's entirely meaningless. Think about what we can do in the situation at hand. Think about how to defeat Seitred, the Margrave of Machaal."

At my words, Noen bowed his head, saying, "My apologies..."

A river flowed between the enemy army and ours. It wasn't a particularly large river, but the current was relatively fast. The question looming over everyone's head was whether we should go ahead and cross the river all at once or stay put and wait.

I tried having my vassals discuss the matter, but their opinions were all over the place. Some said we should wait because the enemy was too strong, while some questioned the usefulness of waiting when we were on an expedition. The debate was a bit too theoretical.

There hadn't been any big wars recently, so they all must've gotten rusty. Before, they had been more desperate to survive.

As it happened, the plan was already settled to begin with. If someone had a better idea, I intended to switch to that, of course.

"No more ideas, everyone?"

At that, a hand went up from quite far back. It was Ortonba the dwarf. Some of my vassals eyed him, wondering who he was. The size of his territory was much smaller than that of my most powerful vassals.

"I believe we should wait. Then if we erect a simple fence and take defensive positions, we can dampen the force of their cavalry charge."

"Even if we dampen their charge somewhat, we're getting hit there, aren't we? How the hell are we supposed to switch to attacking? Once they've come that far, it's over either way, right?" objected Orcus of the Red Bears.

Indeed, that would be the normal way to understand it. If you waited for the enemy at a fence, by the time the fence did its job, the cavalry was already upon you.

"We then shoot them with our guns." Ortonba took out an iron tube. Compared to what I'd seen the first time, it appeared substantially improved.

"Ooh, it looks like you made an awful lot of those," noted Laviala. "I tried one out once before, although I must say I felt a bit conflicted when you said it's stronger than a bow." As an Archer, Laviala must not have been thrilled about a weapon that might take her job.

"These guns will penetrate armor as easily as paper. If your men keep firing from behind the fence whenever they have a shot, it'll work out. The closer the enemy is, the worse their wounds will be."

"Hah! That's gotta be a joke, right?" Apparently, to a war hawk like Orcus, this weapon seemed dubious. To be fair, it hadn't done any real work on a battlefield yet.

"No, Mr. Orcus, this is quite terrifying." This time, Laviala was the one recognizing the value of firearms. "It's far more accurate than a bow. It really isn't half bad."

"Oh, you're gonna take his side, huh…? When it's an Archer saying it…I can't argue with that…" Orcus always folded when it came to a woman's advice.

Afterward, Ortonba gave a concrete explanation about firearms tactics. We would set up several fences at random to keep their cavalry regiment from moving as a group. Then we'd destroy them one by one as their horsemen came up individually. Having lost a great deal of striking power, the enemy would be weakened. And since many of the enemy's top vassals would be among them, if all went well, we could inflict enough damage to make further combat impossible for them.

——Ooh, this reminds me of when I dealt a devastating blow to Takeda Katsuyori.

You did mention winning a big victory using these.

——Of course, once I'd forced them to attack, I'd already won. Takeda made the mistake of underestimating my defenses, thinking he just needed to force a breakthrough. They were haunted by Shingen's ghost—Shingen's twilight years were glorious, but gradually Takeda started getting boxed in.

I don't know who Takeda is, but it seems guns definitely made a difference, so I'll give it a try. I'm sure you approve.

The plan to wait with guns for the Margrave of Machaal was practically settled now. My vassals were also starting to feel that the guns would provide us a sweeping victory.

"All right—Ortonba, was it? Show us everything these guns can do! The Red Bears are with you to the end!" Even Orcus was on board at this point.

© Kaito Shibano

"Yes, I have been making improvements to this for a long time now, so I do think it will be a once-in-a-lifetime moment for me. However…I do have just a little concern…" After all that talk before, Ortonba now looked a bit pale.

"Hey, Ortonba, what do you mean?" I hadn't heard anything about this concern.

"It's looking a bit bleak."

"You mean to tell me now that these guns aren't ready for service?"

It had been five years since I'd first employed Ortonba. If he didn't have something ready to be deployed in battle, it was definitely too late now.

"No, I meant literally. The clouds are very dark. Actually, it's already starting to rain, isn't it…"

Oh, so that was what he'd meant…

Just then I heard the *drip-drop* sound of rain outside. The clouds were thick, too, so who knew when it would stop?

Rain was a weakness of guns. If they couldn't ignite, they'd be reduced to mere iron pipes.

"Laviala, do you know much about weather?"

Elves had a great deal of knowledge about natural phenomena.

"Let's see… Umm, at worst, this might go on for over two days. That's about how gloomy the sky is. When it's this bad, I don't think there will be much light coming through…"

In other words, we had no choice but to hold out until we could use our guns.

"Ahh, so that's the problem! I see! In that case I'll go and stop these Machaal bastards myself!" Orcus exclaimed. "We just attack 'em with all we got, and then when the weather clears up we suddenly pull back! Once we do that, they should all come attack us. Then we hit 'em hard with our guns."

Orcus's plan sounded desperate, but it was the most realistic plan we had. It wasn't clear whether we could keep our lines extended that far until the rain stopped, but if we didn't go on the offensive, we couldn't buy time in the first place.

"All right, who wants to go out?" I asked. "It will be treacherous, but I want you to cross the river and hit them with your best shot. Naturally, I'll give you an ample reward."

Noen and Meissel added their opinions, as Orcus had before.

"It's not that frightening. These kinds of battles are all we've ever fought. In fact, I thought this was normal for us."

"I agree with Sir Noen. As part of Your Excellency's extended clan, I shall risk my life to serve you!"

I certainly had no complaints about my men's offensive capability. If the enemy could scatter these guys, we would've had to retreat anyway.

"All right, I want the vanguard to go ahead and move out. Those of you using guns, be sure you can operate them without issue. If you're unlucky enough to miss your shots, the enemy will cut you to ribbons when they're through."

◇

Thus, the battle between me and Seitred, the Margrave of Machaal, began. Seitred's army reportedly numbered about six thousand—no match for mine, but quite a lot for someone calling himself a margrave. It meant the surrounding lords, for practical purposes, also gave their allegiance to the Margrave of Machaal.

We numbered about ten thousand, as I'd had to leave a number of troops in Maust Castle and the royal capital. In fact, I'd even lent men to the Nistonia clan to help them keep watch on the surrounding area.

"When it comes to expeditions, I expect it's still not practical to overwhelm the enemy with numbers?" Laviala was waiting quietly in the fort for her turn to fight. She was touching one of the guns.

"They won't come straight at us on the plains, after all. The challenges are more than numbers can solve."

"But couldn't you have easily mobilized about twenty thousand? With your power now, I'm sure even faraway lands would have been no problem."

"I could. But the time I could use them would be far shorter." I tore apart some bread and stuck it into my mouth. It wasn't very good-quality bread, so it quickly dried my mouth out. "If the war dragged on, there wouldn't be nearly enough food. Then, when we had to get food locally, we'd earn the ire of the locals, and I'd only have more enemies."

"Ah, I see…" She stopped moving her hand over the gun.

"We're the king's soldiers—we can't go around pillaging everywhere. We are more than mere squabbling petty lords. We carry a completely different burden."

All was fair in war. It was kill or be killed. That was a fact, but whether you could get away with saying it out loud was another matter. If kingdom troops started attacking farming villages, the Northlands would certainly unify to defy the kingdom. That was the one thing I wanted to avoid.

"You sure do think about a lot, Lord Alsrod." Laviala's smile gave me courage, just as it always had since long ago.

Recently, I'd thought my daughter was gradually starting to look more and more like Laviala. I wanted to make it so my daughter would be called princess by the time she was of age. I might have killed many, many people, but I still thought my kids were adorable.

"Frankly, it'd be easier for me if I just took out every enemy that crossed my path, but it's just not practical."

"That's all right. You like hatching plots, too." That was quite a way to put it. "By the way, Lord Alsrod." She turned gloomy. "Do you think Miss Seraphina's clan really will attack us…? Will we have to fight them…?"

"Laviala, let's focus on beating the enemies in front of us right now."

"I'm sorry," Laviala apologized.

"By now, our comrades are performing the dance of life and death to buy time so we can use our guns. Even if there's a rebellion, we have to win against the margrave first."

"That's true. I'll do what I can, too!"

Orcus, Noen, and Meissel were all men of valor who had long fought on the front lines. I didn't think they'd lose very easily, but the enemy was just past the river. Since they'd be fighting in the enemy's land on top of being exhausted, they had to be prepared for a fairly tough battle.

Once in hostile territory, they just needed to hold out. Extending too far would be too risky. Whatever happened, I wanted to create a deadlock in the spot where I was ostensibly pushing.

The rain was coming down pretty strong. Definitely not the weather for using firearms.

——You look frustrated. That's quite rare for you.

Oda Nobunaga was acting cocky. *Not being out there on the battlefield makes me uneasy.*

——You're destined to be a conqueror, so you should act like you're in charge. Going out in front all the time, as you always have, is the wrong way to fight. You're not fleeing back home.

I understand the reasoning. Of course, you're the one who actually gave me powers that made me want to go fight.

——I didn't exactly choose to be a profession myself. In fact, I feel it is decidedly inconvenient. And now Akechi Mitsuhide and Sen no Rikyuu are professions, too. It would be no laughing matter if that Margrave of Machaal fellow's profession turned out to be something like Takeda Shingen.

I asked Oda Nobunaga about something I'd been wondering about.
Tell me about this Takeda Shingen. I think you mentioned him a few times before.

——What's this sudden change in attitude? I suppose there's no reason for a profession to begrudge a mortal, though. Very well.

Takeda Shingen was a hero born in a mountainous land. His skill in war was uncanny. It wasn't all of his army, but part of his elite troops fought on horseback, supposedly.

I asked him about Takeda Shingen for a while; the man seemed somehow similar to my enemy Seitred.

——Of course, I had far loftier political ideas than him, so the Takeda clan was destroyed during his son's reign. He made enemies of both me and Houjou, boxing himself in.

I don't know about his political ideas, but I see Takeda Shingen was pretty competent, at least. I wonder if my men are all right after charging in.

After some time, a less favorable report came from the rappa Yadoriggy. She startled Laviala, who was still there, but that was inevitable. It was clearly that urgent.

"Sir Orcus's troops are struggling against the enemy and need to withdraw."

"I see. That means I'll have to ready a reserve brigade to go in until the weather clears."

"The strongest of our enemies is Seitred's younger sister, Talsha. Word is that she is much younger, though—still twenty-one."

Now that she mentioned it, I thought I'd heard of a female brigadier, but I hadn't expected she'd be that good.

"Originally, she married the son of one of his most powerful vassals, and ever since her husband died three years ago, she has been managing one of the brigades he'd commanded."

Losing to the margrave would be one thing, but I sure didn't want to lose to his little sister.

The rain was still going strong. If we were attacked now, our defenses wouldn't be ready.

"Lord Alsrod, I'll go fight!" exclaimed Laviala.

"All right, don't let me down. But I can't leave this to my wife alone, you know." I sprang to my feet. "I'll go, too. They'll think twice about attacking when I'm done with them."

◇

The river water was quite cold. *This sure is the Northlands, all right*, I thought. The royal capital was much farther south, so I couldn't get used to the temperature here. It'd be understandable if the side that attacked first couldn't bring their strength to bear afterward.

I was leading the charge with a mere four hundred troops. It was only meant to support the other forces. Once they were back on their feet, my men would have enough strength to hold their own. Laviala was with me this time.

"Laviala, you don't need to get any closer to the enemy than is necessary. Whatever you do, just shoot them."

"Yes, sir, understood!" Laviala's eyes were more serious than ever before. "I only have one question—is there really a reason this person is following along?"

Ortonba the dwarf was accompanying us, too. He was carefully crossing the river so as not to get his gun wet.

"One use ought to be enough," he said. "Besides, I can't help you understand how good it is if we don't use it a little in actual battle."

It had never occurred to me that we'd be trying out firearms at a time like this.

We joined up with Noen's troops just as they were taking a brutal enemy attack.

"We're here to help, Noen Rowd, just for now!"

"Ah! I am much obliged! I would hate to bring further shame on myself, so I intend to push back full force!"

This should have temporarily raised my men's spirits; however, my appearance alone wouldn't be enough to repel the enemy. Luckily, their apparent emphasis on speed led them to be lightly armored and thus very shootable.

Laviala wasted no time firing her nocked arrow. It went straight through an enemy soldier's chest, right on target.

"My bow is terrifyingly precise—my Archer profession isn't just for show!"

The next shot pierced yet another soldier. The other archers fired their arrows as well, suppressing the enemy onslaught.

"This place will be all right. Noen, keep it up a little longer! We're heading to help Orcus!"

Orcus's troops comprised the most soldiers of all, so if we could stop the enemy here, the rest would take care of itself. Laviala and I both took our men and moved down the battle line.

The main body of Orcus's troops was indeed embroiled in a chaotic melee. They were suffering a fierce enemy assault, as if they'd gone and poked a beehive.

"We need to stop this at its source."

"I'll do it, Lord Alsrod."

Laviala's arrow threw one man off his horse at the back of the enemy line. However, this time their numbers were many. It would be difficult to weaken their advance with our brief strike.

"I think I can kill about thirty if I go in."

"It's too dangerous! And I won't be able to use my bow!"

Laviala stopped me. Right, of course—since she was using a projectile weapon, I couldn't be on the front line. In that case, my role had to be to boost friendly morale.

From Orcus's troops, I could already hear their leader's deep voice booming out, "No retreating, even in death! Retreat means eternal shame!" He must've heard I was here. He was so transparent.

——This is utterly reckless. Coming yourself to such a perilous battlefield... Don't you dare get yourself killed. If you lose your life here of all places, it'll be no laughing matter for your profession.

He was right, but staying on the sidelines the entire time just wasn't to my taste.

Laviala's attack was working reasonably well, but the margrave's general who commanded the nearby troops must've noticed many of his men had fallen to arrows from a new angle. This time the enemy had enough numbers to break up our attack.

The enemy general seemed to have ordered, "Attack those archers!" Of course, to be honest, I mostly couldn't make it out, as it was in Northlands-speak. Aside from some high officials like the margrave, most of them probably couldn't even talk in capital-speak.

It looked like they numbered about a hundred and fifty. Their tactic was that the general charged in on horseback followed by foot soldiers. Their horses had very dark brown coats and looked significantly larger than ours. Machaal Prefecture was a center of horse breeding.

"Ah! Everyone! Please aim for their general!" Laviala was now in a rush, too. The archers fired their arrows, but the enemy general ducked, evading the volley. He seemed pretty good.

"This is bad... He's just going to plow right into us..." I put a hand on my scabbard. Hand-to-hand combat was somewhat dangerous, but that seemed to be our only way out.

However, Ortonba stepped forward in front of me, gun in hand. He was bent over it so the rain didn't get it wet.

"I can put them down when they're this close. I know which one is their general now, too. No problem."

This definitely was a golden opportunity to test the gun's performance.

"All right. Do it. I'll watch right next to you."

"Lord Alsrod, please don't put too much faith in it!! If it misses, they'll be right on you!" Laviala warned.

Well, if it happens, it happens. I'll give this everything I have.

"Even with this ridiculous stance, I can still hit them."

Baaaaangggg!

A thunderous blast rang out, like the earth itself had torn apart. It was such a tremendous noise, I briefly wondered if I'd died, but that clearly wasn't what had just transpired.

The enemy general fell from his horse and quickly stopped moving. The gun had killed him in one hit.

Cries erupted from the enemy troops. Their general had just died, after all. However, they didn't seem to quite understand just yet what had happened.

"That's right... Everyone, hit them with a volley, please!" Laviala and her archers then fired their arrows once more. The enemy soldiers in front collapsed noisily to the ground.

I was witnessing the moment the situation turned around in front of my eyes. With a single gun, the tide of battle had changed dramatically. The roots that had been feeding the attacking enemy soldiers had been torn up.

The enemy general's pinpoint directions had been what was overwhelming Orcus's men. That general was now dead, and the enemy attack had lost all its energy at the same moment.

"All right! They're just common rabble now! Show them what the Red Bears do best! Push! Push, dammit!" Orcus's voice suddenly got louder. It looked for now like my coming had been worthwhile.

Afterward, Ortonba fired his gun three or so times, and each shot killed another enemy officer. The bullets reached much farther than arrows did.

"It sure does take time to ignite in the rain. We would need clear weather for volley fire."

"At least now we know it's not impossible in the hands of an expert."

It looked like Orcus had driven off the enemy for now, so I left him with orders to hold out until the rain cleared, and we crossed the cold river once again.

Afterward, dusk fell, and I heard that the enemy had pulled back to their camp. To take advantage of this, Orcus and the other frontline regiments returned to our side of the river. For the first day, at least, we'd stopped them.

There was one more turn of events—the rain ceased before nightfall. Perhaps its intensity had made the clouds pass quickly.

"Tomorrow morning will be sunny," Laviala said confidently.

"Indeed. Tomorrow we can finally demonstrate the true worth of these guns."

When the frontline troops got back, I expressed my gratitude and then had them fall back to the rear.

"I would have liked to camp there overnight, but I decided it was impossible given how fatigued my troops were," explained Laviala. "I wanted to hold out until the enemy came to attack again tomorrow."

"If the enemy foolishly comes over to our side of the river, it's no issue. We'll welcome them with our guns."

"But will they come over so easily? I'm sure they know to be afraid, after today."

"I'll put out some good bait. I'm sure the Margrave of Machaal wants to turn this into a clear-cut victory."

During the night I moved the main body of my troops out from the fort.

"I'm moving my headquarters next to the river."

I set up a defensive line close to the banks, deliberately building it to look quite fragile. I had my headquarters set up in front as well. Against this, the enemy could make a quick breakthrough and come for my head—or so they'd believe. If they didn't take the bait, I'd have a detachment cross the river just to lure them, and then I'd pull my men back.

We weren't losing, at least. I'd gotten a good idea of their capabilities, too, so I just needed to finish them in this next fight.

And so the long night ended.

Perhaps because of the higher early-morning temperature, there hung a faint mist, but this too faded as the sun rose.

"We've got some incredibly sunny weather today, Laviala."

"Yes! Let's win and make it even more incredible!"

The two of us exchanged banter back at our camp. Indeed, if we couldn't win, this would turn out to be the most depressing sunshine ever.

Of course, the enemy didn't come in the early morning. I decided to take this time to get fully prepared to meet them. The terrain didn't allow me to place troops behind and have them charge forward. Apparently Oda Nobunaga had been able to go that route, but I couldn't ask for too much here.

The busiest person that day was Ortonba. He went around inspecting the soldiers waiting behind the fences, making sure they could shoot properly. By the way, the fences were set up quite far ahead of where the men were. If they could slow the enemy down, the gunners would have it that much easier.

Just then, Yadoriggy made an appearance. I'd been anticipating her arrival, and I'd deliberately kept only Laviala by my side.

"The Margrave of Machaal has decided to come attack over the river, himself included," she reported.

"Understood. Thanks for letting me know. You look really out of breath, so have a rest."

Her face looked more cold than apathetic, but I'd seen her face so many times now that I could tell she'd been in a rush.

"I will be nearby, so please call me if anything comes up," she said, and she disappeared.

Well, I think we're in for a big battle.

"Laviala, position yourself somewhere you can easily shoot a gun from. The enemy will be on our doorstep before long."

"Yes, sir! I'll shoot them down one by one, starting from the front!"

I wasn't sure how the Archer profession would work with guns, but it had the exact same purpose as a weapon, at least, so surely it would work out.

At last, I could hear a low rumble off in the distance. They were coming from a shallow point in the river. As expected, they seemed to know what terrain was the easiest to cross.

And then, around the time they finished crossing the river, a thunderous blast like the previous day's rang out. The regiment lying in wait on the nearby hillock had fired their guns. It was a bit too far away for me to tell the results, but it didn't matter. The real showdown was yet to come.

I decided to see how Ortonba was faring. I was surely the primary target, too, so if one of their leaders came to me, it'd be easy for Ortonba to shoot them.

"How does it look?" I asked him.

"We have good sights on them, and it's even sunny, so you won't hear me complaining. It already seems to be having an effect."

The sounds of gunfire had already reverberated several times, and the screams had begun.

First, until we drew them close, our focus was to pick them off from up high and far away. They didn't know where the shots were coming from, which instilled a sense of fear. And then when they made it through that attack and came close, the men inside the fences trained their guns on them.

"All right, everyone, fire at will!" I didn't really need to give the command, as they were already under orders to fire, but I shouted anyway to whip them up. I also made absolutely sure to cover my ears.

After the deafening blast, the mounted enemy officers fell noisily to the ground one after another. Of course, we hit their rank-and-file soldiers with gunfire as well. Some among them nearly froze in place out of fear, but our guns showed them no mercy either.

"What the hell kinda weapons are these?!"

"How do we stop them?!"

"Don't get too close!"

Those were just a few of the many shouts I heard following the gunfire. Suffering attacks from a weapon you'd never seen before brought on extraordinary fear. People generally couldn't think straight when confronted with a situation they couldn't explain. That was exactly what I was aiming for.

I could see Laviala sniping with her gun while hidden in some foliage on the hill. Even though she was quite far away, her aim was deadly accurate.

Sure enough, the real star was Ortonba, who took down soldiers quite far off with every shot. Maybe that was why none of their men were any longer trying to break through the fences in front of us—those who had tried to force their way through had all fallen.

We had totally destroyed the enemy cavalry brigade's momentum. At that point, this battle was ours.

The enemy's only hope for victory lay in breaking through our defensive screen, but they almost certainly didn't have the strength left to pull that off now. My opponent's worst enemy was fear. Charging in was impossible with doubt in your heart.

"I guess their attack is finally over. In that case, I might as well take everyone to mop them up."

I hadn't yet seen the margrave. The high percentage of officers who had died in the front had probably kept him from coming out.

However, one of the margrave's units came charging. Though their comrades had fallen, their commanding general wasn't down yet.

I could tell someone important had arrived, given the shift in the atmosphere.

"I am Talsha Machaal, sister of the Margrave of Machaal! Prepare yourself, Alsrod Nayvil!"

Ahh, his famously courageous sister.

With her wavy hair streaming in the breeze, she charged toward me.

"Shit! I said stop! Reckless bitch!" Ortonba shot her horse, which fell over, but Talsha leaped off and headed straight for me. Even as her foe, I was impressed. She was dead set on coming for my head.

I felt a rush of excitement. "No one shoot this woman! I'll take her myself."

This battle was ours, after all. Why not have a little fun?

I drew my sword and stood in front of Talsha.

"You called for me, and here I am. Why did you charge into a lost battle?"

© Kaito Shibano

"Shut your mouth! If I retreated now, my clan would be finished, whether the battle was won or lost! And I'd rather fight than turn tail!"

"I see. I can't say you're wrong."

Talsha's sword was straight as an arrow, with no deviation—a weapon befitting someone coming here.

"It's a pity you're my enemy, with a sword like that."

"Apparently, my profession is that of a famous warrior—Takeda Shingen!"

Takeda Shingen? Isn't that who Oda Nobunaga was talking about?!

——All right, Alsrod, fight with all your might! And win at any cost! I want to know what it feels like to win against Shingen one-on-one, too!

This isn't about you! And not fighting this woman simply isn't an option to begin with. Besides, even if this is a duel, she's already exhausted.

"Alsrod! Your head is mine!"

The woman calling herself Talsha swung her hefty sword down at me. It was a full-force swing, far stronger than you'd expect from a woman. I countered it with the Stroke of Justice, but the shock went through my hands. My big, gnarly sword was able to stop it, but had I been wielding something more modern and mass-produced, I might've been sliced into ribbons.

"Definitely not a refined attack, but the brutality may be enough."

"Do not mock me! Your royal-capital swordplay is so weak! You people just use an extension of ceremonial swordfighting, after all!"

My swordplay wasn't anything I'd learned in the capital, but the capital lords might very well fight like Talsha said. Most of them disdained going out into the middle of the battlefield, for one thing. Talsha's swordplay, on the other hand, was meant only to kill her foes. And that's what made this fun.

I felt like a petty rural lord once more. Had I ever gone in this close to enemy generals?

I laughed in spite of myself, and Talsha shrank back in fear.

Ahh, I guess even the Northlands doesn't have many people who can enjoy a situation like this. But whatever the reason is, once you're afraid, you've lost.

"Now it's my turn!"

Using my whole body, I swung my blade sideways as hard as I could. This old sword was intended to be used with the wielder's full body weight.

Talsha also countered with her sword. My swing wasn't something so fast it couldn't be met. However, whether it could be stopped was another matter.

Talsha's sword was no match for mine—it flew off in an arc!

"How's that for a heavy attack?"

The fight was over; I'm sure everyone had assumed so. In fact, cheers erupted from my side.

However, the fight still hadn't gone out of Talsha's eyes. You absolutely mustn't let your guard down before people with eyes like hers.

Talsha immediately drew a short sword, no longer than about half a jarg at most. It looked like she wasn't going to bend her knee as long as she could fight.

"I shall defeat you, Alsrod, no matter what it takes! Then my clan shall rise like never before!"

"Rise? How ridiculous. I'm sorry, but your domain is much too far away to rule the kingdom. You won't accomplish anything from such a distance."

"Even if we can't rule the kingdom, we can rule three or four prefectures. My plan is to form a federation of multiprefectural lords!" shouted Talsha. She then swiped at me with her short sword.

I felt such power from the impact that I could hardly believe it came from a short sword. This woman boasted exceptional strength.

Something much stronger than that affected me, however. There was someone besides me in this realm who had big plans.

I didn't know if it was realistic, but the most profitable thing for great rural lords would be shared rule with other great lords. They could probably gobble up plenty of smaller lords on their own, but they would hit a wall eventually. I intended to subjugate those great lords by force to achieve unification, but it made sense that someone would plan to form a coalition.

"Alsrod! Indeed, you are mighty, but ultimately you built all of this in just your own generation! When you die, the world will fall into chaos once more! So that gives me any number of openings to exploit!"

What Talsha spoke of was no silly fantasy; I knew that better than anyone. That was why this woman was doing everything she could to come kill me. It wasn't particularly to protect her domain or anything simple like that.

In my mind, Oda Nobunaga was shouting, *"Don't you dare ease up on her! She will stop at nothing to achieve her goals—be that driving out her parents or murdering children!"* Indeed. People who could forsake everything for their goals were formidable.

I swung my sword with all my might as well.

"You're not half bad, Talsha!"

"Enough! I'll kill you here and now!"

"Submit to me! Your true worth is waiting in your future!"

Of course, Talsha shouted "I'm nobody's fool!" and thrust her short sword at me.

However, I sensed the power behind her sword had diminished. After all, I could help her realize her goals. Talsha could have a place in the new realm I would rule.

I snatched Talsha's sword hand and twisted it upward.

"N—agh…"

Her sword fell to the ground. She was now entirely powerless.

"I can't kill a defenseless woman, you see. I'm taking you prisoner."

"Do as you will. But if you disrespect me, I'll bite your tongue right off…!"

Her spiteful remarks actually made this even more satisfying.

The battle was completely one-sided after that. Enemy morale fell dramatically.

"She's been captured!"

"Retreat!"

More and more members of the enemy force were beginning to panic. Just as I thought—her Takeda Shingen profession must have had some effect like greatly raising the unity of allies. It seemed the Margrave of Machaal's strength lay not in himself, but in his outstanding commanders.

The battle had ended in a great victory for us and our guns. The Margrave of Machaal had no choice but to withdraw his troops to his home castle for now. He likely predicted they'd be wiped out otherwise. And he was right to think so.

"Let's chase them down and end them now!" Laviala suggested, but I declined.

"No need. All we need to do now is build a fort here and hold our ground. At the very least, recovery is impossible for them now."

"But even though we won, we still haven't taken their territory."

"This is a list of the primary enemy casualties this time. You'll understand when you look at it."

I could immediately tell Laviala was shocked at the numbers.

"We absolutely slaughtered them with our guns. Their clan hasn't gone extinct—their children or brothers will probably take over—but even so it'll take ages for them to function properly again. Of course, history won't wait that long for them."

Soon, the petty lords who were only following the Margrave of Machaal's lead would realize their days were numbered and abandon him before running to my side.

"Besides, we have a hostage."

*　　*　　*

"If you work for me as a general, I'll let the Machaal clan survive. This may not be quite what you'd envisioned, but I'll allow them the possibility to exist as a great lord over several prefectures." I'd ducked out of the victory banquet to see Talsha where she was being held prisoner.

"It pains me to do so, but it seems there's no other way... To think I'd ever end up bowing to you..." Talsha still looked disgusted, but she then sighed deeply as if to forget it. "I will fully comply. If you're going to treat me as a general, do let the other generals know right away."

She changed her attitude fast. She must've still had a desire to fight.

Thus, this expedition ended in success for the moment, but the real fight was still to come.

The day after the banquet, a messenger came to me on horseback. I'd had him put on a blue sash beforehand, so I instantly knew why he had arrived. The sash was there to let me know what had happened just by the color.

"Marquess of Brantaar Ayles Caltis and Count of Olbia Brando Naaham have both raised their armies!"

So my father-in-law and brother-in-law were challenging me to a fight. I'd expected as much. Now that they had made their intentions clear, I would crush them both.

What followed, however, was entirely unexpected.

"Also...it appears financial officer Fanneria has joined their ranks...as has at least one of the lords near Maust Castle..."

Fanneria was a werewolf I'd originally hired when he was a merchant. However, after I'd advanced into the royal capital, he'd had fewer opportunities to shine. Since I was using more and more such ex-merchants—like Yanhaan, for example—his work had become mostly centered on Fordoneria Prefecture.

I clicked my tongue with frustration. I didn't know who had sprung this first—whether it was Ayles or Brando or even Fanneria—but it appeared they intended to annihilate me. But to think there would be an uprising near my domain's capital as well—I'd never anticipated it.

"I accept their challenge. That's why I came so far north, after all."

END

As one of the largest castles in all the kingdom, Maust's had several moats. Naturally, they were defensive structures just like those in all other castles, but in peacetime they played another role—a place of relaxation for the castle's denizens.

Several people had cast their fishing lines in the sections where the activity was permitted. Since the moats were sourced from the nearby river, fish were swept down with the current. These were by no means swamp fish that stank of mud. With the proper cooking and preparation, they were quite tasty. I could say so from experience, as the castle cooks had served me fish taken from the moat on a few occasions.

In several spots were wooden stairs that descended into the moat, as even moats needed maintenance from time to time, including having the mud cleaned out. Because they were wooden, the stairs could be removed when the castle was attacked.

As I was taking a stroll, I stopped in my tracks upon glimpsing a strange figure. I couldn't help but think it looked like that familiar pink-haired creature I knew so well.

Is that really Fleur?

I quietly took a good peek. No question about it. My concubine Fleur was down on the lower steps, right where they met with the water, stooped slightly with knees bent.

What is she doing? Drowning herself? No, then she'd jump down from the top of the moat.

When I looked closer, though, something glinted briefly. Fleur was grasping a knife.

Surely she can't be contemplating suicide...?

I shuddered. As Fleur was already holding the knife, frightening her would be counterproductive. Quietly going down the stairs and grabbing her would be better. Ever so silently, I crept closer...

...and just then, she plunged the knife into the water.

"Yes! Gotcha!"

Fleur's uncharacteristically jovial cry startled me. "Got what?" I murmured.

She wheeled around in surprise—and surprised me as well. Stuck on her knife was a river fish.

$$\diamond$$

We sat on the moat's edge, just above the staircase. Falling off would cause a scene, but neither of us was that clumsy.

"I suppose I gave you a fright, didn't I?" Fleur smiled awkwardly as she looked down. "Actually, with all the mountains where I come from, I often used to play in mountain streams as a child. Perhaps I wanted to relive my childhood just now."

"I see. So you were a tomboy, huh? When I first met you, you were already an elegant lady of a fallen people, so I never got that impression."

"Yes, I suspect I was working hard to win your sympathy." Fleur forced a laugh, so it must've been at least partially a joke. Of course, with her intelligence and perseverance through so many trials, it would be no surprise if Fleur came up with something like that on the spot.

"Please be careful in the Northlands war." She gently placed her hand over mine.

The departure date for the Northlands was only a few days away now. As I made a show of authority to Seitred, the Margrave of Machaal, it would also serve the purpose of luring out anyone considering rebellion.

The risk was great, but I needed to get my hands dirty sooner rather

© Kaito Shibano

than later if I wanted to corner the former king's faction in earnest hereafter.

"In a few years, I'll have made things peaceful enough you can enjoy the water any time you like. Until then, I want you to watch over this castle for me. You're my wife, but I also genuinely consider you my castle commander when I'm away at war."

"Can you please make sure not to forget what you've just told me?" Fleur smiled at me enticingly.

Before the moment passed, I immediately pressed my lips to hers. I was sure I'd heard birds chirping up until a moment ago, but I no longer noticed them; they might as well have disappeared.

"Thank you, dear."

"It's pretty silly to thank your husband."

"Well then, can I ask you not to take any more lovers during the Northlands war?"

Her elegant smile put me at a loss for words.

"Er... Well, you never know how things will turn out... I can't promise anything..."

"You don't need to give an honest answer. Just make something up for me." Fleur pinched the back of my hand a bit.

Yes, it did hurt, but somehow that didn't bother me.

Afterword

Long time no see. This is Kisetsu Morita.

The second volume of *A Mysterious Job Called Oda Nobunaga* is out! Thank you so much!

In very broad terms, this is the capital-bound arc. I think historical figures everywhere took this sort of approach—going into the capital together with a noble who is in a position to become king, just like Oda Nobunaga. Alsrod likewise enters the royal capital and becomes regent, the most powerful of vassals.

However, in Japan's Sengoku period, holding power in Kyoto merely amounted to a hegemony over the capital region, since those with any authority in Kyoto were ousted over and over again. And so Alsrod is still stuck having to fight his enemies, not to mention fighting desperately to secure his power in the capital area to begin with. This is what the second volume is about!

Also, since becoming regent would likely lead to having more wives, there are even more enchanting girls drawn by Mr. Kaito Shibano in the second volume! I hope you enjoyed these as well!

You may have seen the ads by now, but…

A Mysterious Job Called Oda Nobunaga is now slated for a manga adaptation! It will be published via Gangan GA, just like the manga adaptation of *I've Been Killing Slimes for 300 Years and Maxed Out My Level*, the light novel version of which shares the same GA Novel label as the book you're reading now. (Please take a look at *I've Been Killing Slimes for 300 Years...* as well!)

Honestly, when I was contacted about a manga adaptation for *A Mysterious Job Called Oda Nobunaga*, I called the editor to make sure I really could get a second work adapted—that this wasn't some kind of mistake. When they confirmed it was true, I was absolutely thrilled! I will announce more detailed information once I have it!

In this volume, the unification of the kingdom is getting closer and closer, but the manga adaptation is just getting started! I hope you'll cheer on Alsrod in his endeavors there as well!

Mr. Kaito Shibano has yet again drawn many truly wonderful illustrations for this book, all of which help motivate me to put out more chapters on Shousetsuka ni Narou! Thank you so much! Well then, let's meet again in Volume 3!

Respectfully yours,

Kisetsu Morita

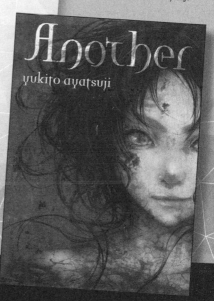

I've Been Killing SLIMES for 300 Years and Maxed Out My Level

It's hard work taking it slow...

After living a painful life as an office worker, Azusa ended her short life by dying from overworking. So when she found herself reincarnated as an undying, unaging witch in a new world, she vows to spend her days stress free and as pleasantly as possible. She ekes out a living by hunting down the easiest targets—the slimes! But after centuries of doing this simple job, she's ended up with insane powers... how will she maintain her low key life now?!

IN STORES NOW!

Light Novel Volumes 1-7

Manga Volumes 1-3

For more information, visit www.yenpress.com